Hittaz Die Every Day

by

Michael Lawrence

Hittaz Die Every Day

ISBN: 978-1-7366158-2-9

Table of Contents

Prologue

* * * * *

Waking up was unlike any other morning. Even though my mind, body, and soul were awake, my broken heart wouldn't allow my eyes to open. It was as if my heart wanted me to stay in the dark forever, block out all the things that went wrong in the past few weeks, afraid to grasp the reality of having to deal with the pain. The hurt was too deep for me to endure. I wanted nothing more than to take back all I heard last night. If I had the power, I would erase last night and the weeks before from my memory. No matter how hard I prayed or how hard I cried, nothing was going to change the facts. My eyes began to flicker. It was becoming harder to keep them closed. I squeezed tight, rolled over onto my stomach, and pulled the covers over my head. Anything to keep the sun's intense shine from forcing my eyes open.

"Fuck, fuck, fuck, fuck, fuck!" I screamed through gritted teeth.

I couldn't believe how life had just thrown me a sucker punch. Fear gripped my heart like it wanted to rip open my chest and remove the organ from me while it was beating. All I could do was scream into my pillow as I remembered the look on my mother's face. She called out to me, waking me from my sleep.

From the tone of her voice, I knew she was mad. I'm far from a saint, but I made sure that the things I did in the streets never found their way into my mother's home. So, what could she be angry with me about? With each step, I tried to imagine what it could be. Still, as I entered her room, I could not have guessed what the issue was. Then, my eyes spotted her tears, which my ears now could hear her cry. Her head was down, but I knew what I was seeing. I wanted to know what it was that caused her so much pain. I started to speak, but my own voice was caught in my throat. Her tears brought tears to my eyes as well. I had to look away, just so I could get my emotions in order. Never had I ever liked to see a woman cry, especially not my mother.

"What's wrong, ma?" I asked trying to sound more like the man I believe I am. My mother didn't speak, she only looked at me through red, sad eyes. She sighed heavily, which seemed to add years to her pretty face. Next, she hit me with a massive bomb. One so powerful, I couldn't hide my emotions any longer.

"Your brother was murdered! They found his body three hours ago—" The tears were flowing again, and her voice broke up with each word. Nothing at that moment made sense to me. I could not believe my brother, Khafil, was dead and gone. He wasn't the type of kid to be out on the streets. He wasn't involved in anything that would take his life behind his actions. I was thinking about how this could be true when my mother's words cut me like a sword.

"It's all your fault!" she cried. Something I did came back to bite me in the ass. Actually, my actions caused my only blood brother to lose his life. His death was on my hands.

"I'm sorry this happened, ma!" I pleaded, hating myself.

"Don't you sorry me! Your brother is lying dead on the street behind something you did. I know good and well, that boy ain't steal no money!" She was livid; her mentioning of money caught my attention quick.

"What money? What are you talking about?"

"Don't play stupid with me." She snapped. "You been acting crazy all night long. Benny calls here sounding like he's been crying. I know this has something to do with you." She stood up before me, close to my face.

"Now I want you to tell the police everything you know and after you do, I want you out of my house!" That was last night, and here it was six in the morning, and I was hiding under my covers like some little kid. I was afraid to leave the house, because I now know that Chrome and Black knew I robbed their warehouse.

Chapter One

* * * * *

When I was a lot younger than my 19 years, my family would make my older cousin, Perry, take me everywhere he went. At times, Perry hated to have me following him. There were times when he was happy I was around. I remember one time when he was walking around the downtown area. Just so happens that a local crew from another part of town was downtown shopping as well. The issue was, local crews at this time in Bridgeport, CT were at each other's throats. This particular day, Perry did not want me following him, so I mostly played in the background. Even though I was following him, I was far behind because I was looking through every window I passed. Back then, it's safe to say, I was unaware of a lot of things, but Perry was not. He had known that two guys were following him, which was the reason he had been walking so fast. Also, the reason I never saw him make the quick left down the alleyway. By the time my young ass noticed he was gone, it was too late.

Even at 12, I was never one to panic. I knew where I was and how to get back home, so I continued to walk up ahead. Upon arriving at the alleyway, I looked inside because it was more instinct than anything else. To my surprise, I saw my cousin in the middle of a fight with two guys. I was not a big kid at all, but

I still was one to fight when provoked. I ran down that alley as fast as my legs would allow. The whole way, I'm searching my surroundings for something I could use as a weapon. The closer I got to the situation, the more I realized Perry had one guy on the ground choking him.

The other guy was trying his hardest to help his friend, but Perry had him kept at a distance with his left hand, pushing him backwards. I found no weapon to use, but that did not stop me from flying through the air like I was Bruce Lee's last student. The high-flying karate kick to the kid's back sent him falling forward and me backwards. I was on my feet just as quick, as my prey, but I was quicker. I kicked him in the face then fell to the ground next to him. I climbed on top, just like I saw Perry doing. I grabbed his neck with two hands, squeezed tightly. I was yelling. "You thought you was gone jump my fam, huh? Thought he was by himself, huh?" Each time I shouted a question, I was instinctively shaking his head. I glanced at Perry and caught him smiling at me. When he punched his prey, I punched mine. Needless to say, when we were done with them two they were fucked up! From then on, Perry would teach me things about the streets.

I remember one time he was out on the block selling crack cocaine. I just happen to walk by him in the middle of a sell. He saw me, see him pass off the crack vial exchange for a fresh twenty-dollar bill. He said nothing, but when he got home, he came through his room door, saw me on the bed chillin. He pulled me up by my arm and threw me against the wall.

"If you tell my mom what you saw, imma whoop yo ass!" His eye were bloodshot red and the way he pushed me against the wall had me tight. If I thought I could whoop him, I would have rushed his big ass.

"I wouldn't tell on you, dummy!" I shouted.

"Well, you bet not! And if I ever see you smoking or selling that shit, Imma whoop yo ass right where you stand." He let go of my shirt and I was happy too. Even though he had released me I still wanted to punch him in the face.

"I would never smoke that shit." I told him after rethinking my attack on his ass.

"Betta not!" Perry countered. It was like that always for us. Love/hate, back and forth. All day every day I would try to show him that I was just as cool as him. He would just treat me like a kid. I loved and hated it. I looked up to Perry, so his approval was something I wanted. I would smile when my aunt told me to go with him. Every time, he would trick me into doing something I shouldn't do. He thought I would get in trouble, then he could go off without me, but my aunt knew her son, so we both would get in trouble. She would whoop me, then turn around and whoop Perry's big ass for letting me do whatever dumb thing I did. Of course, after those whoopings, Perry would be even madder at me. I didn't care though, I was mad at him too!

"Come on, wake up!" Perry kept slapping me on my leg and yelling at the same time.

"Come on what, man? It's too early for you to be playing dumb ass games." I was groggy and I wanted nothing more than to be left alone so I could sleep more.

"I got some girls for us! So get dressed and let's go!" He demanded, prodding me on.

" Girls?" I asked, dumbfounded.

"Yeah! Unless you too gay to fuck with girls." Perry jabbed, as if he was stating the obvious.

"I ain't gay!" I jabbed back at him.

"Then get your ass up!" Even though I didn't want to go, I got up. I took a shower, which Perry thought I was taking too long doing. That only made me take even longer, just to piss him off.

"Stop playing with your dick and let's go!" Perry was yelling through the bathroom door. He was really pissing me off, so I really took my time. When I was done, I could see he was livid with me. Now I know I mentioned before that Perry couldn't leave the house without me. I knew this and played on it. I knew he had told me a lie making it sound like he had a girl for me, when he had only the one for himself. Therefore, he gon wait on me! Two hours later, I was dressed and ready to go.

We had to take the bus to the south end. Once we got to the south end, we walked over to the apartment building where we were supposed to be meeting two Spanish chicks. Bunny ears on the two! *Two cousin dating two cousin*, as he said. We took the elevator up to the seventh floor. We came to 704, Perry knocked, and then we were blessed by a beautiful Spanish girl and a smile. I could see exactly why Perry wanted to hurry up and get to her. She was beautiful and the way she was dressed made me want to go back home take a shower and touch my damn self. She was bad!

"Hey, Perry!" She greeted.

"What's good, ma! Ya cousin here yet?" He asked her.

"Yeah, she back there!" She moved out the way so we could come inside.

"Jessica this is my cousin, Mecca. Mecca, this is Jessica" Perry was saying, but I was too busy watching Jessica's ass walk across the room. The whole time, I was thinking she was the chick my cousin came to see but I was wrong, she was for me. I was glad and my lil man inside my jeans jumped up and gave my pants a high five.

"How you doing, Jessica?" I asked in my smoothest voice ever.

"I'm good, you from around here?" she asked. Her Spanish accent sounded great to my young ears.

"Naw, I'm from Long Island." I responded.

"New York?" She asked me.

"Yeah." She was too damn pretty but a lot easier to talk to than I had expected. I was happy to find out she wasn't stuck up like most girls that were as pretty as her.

"Y'all play nice!" Then Perry disappeared to the back room. I talked with Jessica for an hour and Perry had still been in the back room. I guess Jessica could see me looking so she decided to tell me, "They back there fucking." The way she said it with so much ease made me think that she thought it was a regular thing. To be fucking! To be honest, at this point in life I was still a virgin, so hearing Perry was fucking I was beginning to think I should be fucking too. Again, as if she could read my mind.

"It's okay, we can go outside if you want to. We don't have to... you know. do the do!" She stared at me with a smile so sexy I couldn't resist.

"It's okay with me! I mean... I don't mind if we... you know, do the do!" I was stuttering a little, not a lot, but just enough to where I could see Jessica was laughing at me. Now, I hate to be the butt of someone's joke, so I pulled her close to me. I closed my eyes, poked out my lips and kissed her dead on her nose. She laughed even more than before, but I was laughing too. Then out of nowhere she kissed me on my lips, tongue, and all.

"Let's go outside for a while, let them do them. If you still want to do the do when we get back, I say we kick them out, so we can be alone." Her words were sweet and her accent had me wrapped around her finger. Day one and she had me following orders like some lost puppy she found in the woods. " Okay!" Outside, we went to the deli to get some Hero's made.

After the deli, we went to the playground, sat on the bench to talk some more. Time flew by, we talked, swinged, and I actually got to know her. I realized I liked her even more than I did when I first arrived. She was two years older than me, and she did have a boyfriend. Kind of! She explains that her cousin also had a boyfriend, they were broken up, but the dude just wouldn't let go. When I asked about her boyfriend, she told me he was in prison.

"Damn!" I said as a response.

"Yeah, he killed someone, so he has to do twelve years." She said, laying it thick.

"Twelve years, that's a lot of time!"

"I know." Jessica replied.

"Well, I don't know about you, but I think I'm ready to do the do!" I joked, but we both knew how serious I was.

"Let's go!" She agreed smiling at me. It didn't take much for me to hop up and begin to walk away with her. The walk back was a quiet one but, the silence was broken up by the sirens and all the people gathered around the apartment building. Jessica and I both faced each other and then shrugged it off. We both knew how it goes down in the hood, so we continued to push our way through the crowd. Nosy neighbors, police, and ambulance cart pushers were everywhere. The elevator was clear, so we hurried on. It wasn't until we got out on the seventh floor that my heart began to skip. In moments like this where, the action seems closer to home than it should, you just pray that it's no one you know or love. In my case, things were worse than I would like to admit. The cart pushers were pushing a gurney out from 704. Jessica ran past me and maybe I did too, but if I was running, I was moving slow as hell. I heard her scream and then she flew through the apartment door pushing people out her way. I knew then that her departure wasn't one of despair, it was one of relief, followed by hope. The face under the gurney I knew well. I loved him like a brother even though he was my cousin. Perry was shot clearly in the head. Most of his face missing. The officers tried to move me away from him.

"I'm his cousin!" I screamed at them.

"Can you tell us his name?" I was in a daze. I was hoping and praying this was not Perry, but nothing was going to change the facts. To see his body laid out, had me furious. I was mad at the cops, I was mad at Jessica, I was mad at that bitch of a cousin, Jessica held screaming inside the apartment. Most of all, I was mad at myself, I should have never left him there alone. Maybe I could have saved his life. Or maybe I could have been sitting on a second gurney behind his. There was only one thing I was certain, Perry was dead. I did not know who it was that shot my cousin, but I do know he got away. I never did get a chance to do the do with Jessica. I couldn't stand to look at her. She reminded me of how easy it was for me to leave my family out to dry by himself. I blamed her and her dumb ass cousin for his death. A masked man? She told the police! That bitch knew who it was that ran up in there busting his gun. For that, I made sure that my female cousin's put an ass whippin to both them hoes and hell no they ain't hide behind no mask!

Chapter Two

* * * * *

It's something about death that makes you grow up quicker. After Perry's death, I began to look at life differently. I started to care less about my actions and more about living life the way I wanted. Perry opened my eyes to the fact that life is shorter than we expect. One day we're here, the next day, we could be gone. So, I decided to get mine before niggaz started stashin! I was going to live my life like there is no tomorrow. At 13, I started smoking weed with my cousin Jt. We would wait until late night and hang our heads out the window when we smoked. My aunt was cool, but she wasn't that damn cool. We both were getting ass whippins if she caught us, but that didn't stop us. We never got caught, but every time we smoked, we made sure that this time wouldn't be the first time. Since Perry was gone, I started to spend my summers off from school with Jt. It was the same custom, Jt had to take me everywhere he went, only Jt didn't mind me following him. He would go on about his day like it was nothing to him. He didn't hide what he was doing from me. He actually showed me how to do things.

We left his house and walked straight to the corner where he sold his drugs. I came along, and from a short distance, I would watch his moves. He was making so much money in such short time, I began to wonder what it would be like if I was selling drugs too. All he did was stand there, wait, people walked up, he gave them a vial, they gave him cash. Simple! Jt would send me to the store while he made the money. I would run to the weed man, buy the smoke, come back and we would get so high out there it wasn't funny. I was like the errand boy. At that time, I didn't mind! I was on the scene and smoking weed all day, nothing else mattered to me. I saw other kids my age playing basketball and things, but I wasn't interested in perfecting my jump shot. I was trying to perfect how to sell a crack rock.

"Jt, why you always wearing the same clothes?" It was something I needed to know. It had never failed with him. Every morning, he would wake up, shower, and throw the same clothes back on. It was crazy to me.

He laughed at first, but he replied, "'Cause these are my stash pants. Plus, ain't no need for me to be out here looking pretty and shit. Imma leave that up to you and them starched up jeans you wear all the time. I'm out here to get money."

"Fuck you, I look good in these jeans!" I protested, feeling like he was clowning me.

"Yeah, well, I wouldn't! Plus, I let my pockets speak for me!" He expressed as he showed me a wad of cash.

"Wow! You making money like that, standing on this hot ass corner?" I asked.

"I told you, I ain't out here trying to be cute like them bum ass niggaz down there." He pointed down the street, referring to the two drug dealers, sitting on the hood of a Benz. I'm looking at them, but, I'm wondering why my cousin didn't have a car. All the money he making, he should have a fly ride too.

"Why you ain't got a car?"

"I do." He gave me a cold answer.

"Yeah, right! I'm with you every day and known you all my life. Only car you got is Auntie's Honda!" I was joking, but dead serious. I knew he had no car. If he did, he would have been pulled it out.

"Goes to show how much you know! Look, cuz,.. It's no need to be so flashy. Dem fools down there, yeah the shit looks good, but trust me, they gon be the first ones in jail and the first ones to tell on the next nigga so they don't go to prison. Me, I ain't getting caught. If I do, I ain't got shit to say. Them flashy ass niggas down there, they weak links."

"I feel you." My voice lost in my own thoughts. He was already serving another crackhead.

"Hey, go grab some weed and some blunts real quick." He gave me the money.

"I'll be back in an hour, since I gotta walk every damn where." Jt laughed, he knew I was only joking. Walking to the 44 store didn't bother me, nor did walking to the weed man bother me. All I cared about was lighting that blunt once I got back. That was the year my mother decided we were moving to North Carolina. Me, moms, and my little brother Khafil, headed down south and I swore up and down I was going to hate it.

That all changed when I met Benny. Benny was the first of my friends I met, who introduced me to Bug, Lil G, and Leroy. From the very first time we met, we all knew we were going to be tight. That summer we did everything together. By the time summer was over, my mom was calling them her sons and their mothers was calling me the same. When school started, I didn't feel like an outsider. I had friends already, I didn't need to make new ones. The few people I did speak to was only because one of my homeboys introduced me—or because I liked to fight, so people tried to stay on my good side. Once, I fought a kid because he was talking about my New York accent. I fought a kid because he called me a pretty boy. Another time, I was fighting because Leroy was talking to a girl and the girl's brother thought he had to big boy Leroy. He pushed Leroy and I Super-Man'd his ass. My attitude was out of control, but no matter how much I acted out in school, I would never disrespect my mother. Truth be told, I was scared to come home those days, I knew I was in trouble. I stayed on punishment so much that my friends would come over and ask my mom could they come be on punishment with me.

Despite my ongoing misbehavior, I always managed to keep my grades up. Which is why, when the summer came, my mother allowed me to go to New York. The first place I went when I got to town, was to see Jt. It felt like forever since the last time I seen him, and I was happy to be back up top. Coming through his room door, I could see nothing had changed with him. His clothes were all on the floor, just like before. When he saw me, I saw he was just as happy as I was. He hopped off the bed, hugged me and then plopped right back down across his bed.

"Damn, cuz it's been a while! How long you in town?" He asked.

"For the summer." I responded.

"Good! We gon have to go out somewhere then. You still smoking?"

"Hell yeah!" I was excited!

"Shiiiit, roll up then. It's some weed in my pants right there."

"Where the blunts at?" I wondered.

"On the dresser." I searched the top of his dresser and found no blunts, I then looked around the room hoping to find some blunts somewhere. There was none.

"Ain't nothing up here!" I told him.

"Damn, we gotta hit the deli then." He said to me.

"Well get yo fat ass up then." My nigga Jt, was still the same. He got up from his bed, stretched, and then just like I knew he would, he grabbed the same jeans he most likely had on the day before. He saw me shaking my head and he just laughed. "Ain't shit changed. I still ain't trying to impress no one." I just shook my head again and laughed.

We were about to walk out the door when my aunt stopped us. She wanted to know where we were going. Jt told her the store. "Be careful and grab me some Newport's." She said as Jt held his hand out for the money. She just waved him off. The whole thing was silent and funny. At least to me, I laughed, Jt did not. Outside, we walked through the parking lot on our way to the path that led to the store. Jt stopped at a car. A piece of junk car, with primer gray paint.

"This you?" I asked, already knowing the answer since he already had his key in the door.

"Yeah! This me!" He was smiling from ear to ear. I just bust out laughing.

"What kind of car you drive?" he asked me.

"I don't have one." I was still laughing.

"My point exactly! Now get in and shut up!"

"Is it safe?" I'm still laughing.

"You can walk!"

"Naw, I'm coming." Now he was laughing! I was surprised to see he had finally bought himself a car. It wasn't the best looking, but it was most definitely his.

"Nigga, you driving like you on the drag strip!" I was beginning to learn why my aunt said to be careful.

"You scared?" He asked.

"Hell nah! I just wanna live to smoke again." I was trying to be cool again. Around him, I always wanted to be his equal. I was three years younger, but still I had to be an equal. I was scared! Jt not only drove fast, he couldn't drive at all. His car may have been ugly, but it was powerful and with power come speed. The car was meant to be on a drag strip. I'm not a car person, so I never knew what kind of car he drove, I just know it was old.

"Aw, nigga, you good!" Jt ignored me and the traffic laws. Thankfully, we made it back safely. We smoked two blunts, and I was glad because my nerves needed it.

Chapter Three

* * * * *

That was the summer Jt introduced me to Anton. Anton was the same age as Jt, but this dude was getting crazy money. First time I met him, he smoked some fire weed with us. Then, when they got down to business, he gave Jt two ounces of crack cocaine. Me, I couldn't keep my eyes off the amount of drugs he actually had. He made no attempts to hide his stash. Right there before me, I was looking at what had to be a kilo of coke. The open drawer provided for me a straight view of all there was to see. I was still bewildered by the amount inside the drawer when Anton handed me a little baggie with the hard rock substance inside.

"What's this? I ain't no smoker!" I was offended by the thought that anyone would assume I smoked crack.

"You bet not be! This a quarter ounce. I see you staring, you might as well get some money while you here!" Anton was speaking, but I was looking at Jt for approval. I didn't know how else to react, but I knew for sure my cousin wouldn't let me go wrong. I saw him shake his head yes, I stuck the baggie in my pocket.

"Thanks!" I said.

"No problem!" Anton said, but he and Jt were back talking just as quickly. Only thing on my mind after that was the fat wad I would have after selling all that crack. We smoked once more before we left. In the car, Jt told me how he and Anton used to be mad cool in school. Then Anton quit school to sell crack and he blew up on the streets. Once that happened, Anton no longer had time for friends. The streets were too demanding, so by the time Jt quit school, Anton was already on top. Jt went to Anton to purchase some drugs to sell, and Anton gave him more than he paid for. Since then, they been getting money out the streets.

"Look, I know you wanna get some money but if my mom finds out she gon kill us both." Jt stated. This was the conversation I had been waiting on the whole ride back. I knew there was no way Jt was going to let me sell dope without the speech of all speeches.

"She ain't gon find out." I tell him trying my best to convince my big cousin that it was cool for me to be on the block slanging crack.

"I know she ain't, cause you won't be selling shit."

"Whaaaat?" I couldn't believe his ass.

"Just give me what you got. Imma throw you some money!" I never sold drugs before, but I've seen it done. Used to watch Perry make sales and bag up coke. I even had my homeboy Bug, in North Carolina, as a teacher. Bug used to steal weed from his brother and then he would bag it and sell some at school. Mostly we smoked it, though.

"How much money?" I wanted to know how much I could get.

"Imma give you two hundred. I just don't want you out there. If something pop off." He cautioned.

"I'm good! I ain't worried bout no shit poppin off! These niggaz don't scare me!" I sounded sure as hell.

Jt laughed at me. "Them niggaz bet not scare you but I ain't talking about them niggaz I'm talking bout them boyz!"

Now, the whole time, I never once had a thought about the police. I was more concerned about someone trying to rob or cheat me. I completely forgot about the police. In my defense, I have never seen the police come around. Jt has been getting money on the same block for so long and had never been arrested I just thought the cops didn't care. My facial expression must have been speaking volumes.

"Ohhh, you thought this shit was legal, huh?" Jt grinned.

"Nah, I just never seen the police fuckin with you." I concluded.

"That's because I'm smart. I know what I'm doing out here. It's ways to doing things. You can't be out here stuck on stupid. Them folks see you and will pick you apart." Jt explained.

"I ain't no dummy!" I had to defend my pride. It was like he was taking shots at me.

"I know you is no dummy but youz a fresh face. When they see you, they going to know exactly what you doing. when they pull up on you what you gon do?"

"Imma run!" I answered, confident Jt would agree.

"Run? Nigga, they will catch you before you get off the block. You don't know your way around here. Even if you did know your way, they just gon keep coming back until they find you."

"By then I won't have nothing on me!" I stated the obvious.

Jt just laughed. " Oh, so you got it all figured out, huh?" Jt teased.

"No, not all but enough to know I can do this and not get caught." I was certain that the little amount of crack I had would be gone so fast, the police won't have time to notice me.

"I can make my quick two hundred dollars and be out the way before they come around."

"Alright! Imma let you rock my corner. Imma play the other side, by the basketball court. That way I can see if some foul shit pop off."

"Cool!" I was excited, they didn't know how they had just created a monster. The whole ride I kept feeling the hard rocks through the plastic baggie. Jt said two hundred, that was good enough for me, I only had thirty to my name. I could use the extra money.

What started out to be one hundred profit was looking more like three-fifty once Jt showed me how to break it down to twenty-dollar rocks. Seeing all those little pebbles and counting the value made me see my big cuz in a different light. This nigga had just tried to cheat me. Clearly, I could see that I would make a lot more than two hundred.

"Man, you said two hundred!" My voice was very accusing, and I meant it to be.

"If I sold it for you, yeah! But since you working it yourself, you making more." He replied.

" A lot more!" I said, shocked.

"Well, not really, you still owe my man Anton. He gonna want two hundred."

"That still leaves me with four hundred dollars' worth of shit. You said two hundred!" Still trying to accuse him of trying to cheat me.

"That's because I was selling the shit for you. I gotta get mine too! Right? Or was I supposed to sell the shit for you for free?" Now I was beginning to understand that he was only trying to split it 50/50 with me. All I could do is laugh.

"Funny nigga you are! You act like you can whoop me or sumthin!" Jt teased me again.

"I know how to fight! But my bad!"

"You good! Just remember to keep that animal inside you for them niggaz who really out to cheat you! You show them no mercy!"

Chapter Four

* * * * *

A fter that money came with ease! One couldn't stop it's like he had a disease!

It was no secret, I was hooked. That Slick Rick song was my anthem. I would hit the block early. Some days, I had to go see Anton myself. I was selling out so fast, I would re-up twice some days. I moved up from quarter ounces to ounces. In the shorts weeks of selling drugs, I had some of my own money put up. This is not to mention all the money I spent. I bought new clothes and shoes for school. Clothes for the nights me and Jt went out, plus the weed we smoked constantly. I would be so high sometimes, people would call me Chinese. I didn't care though. I would smile and laugh with my hand out to collect my dough. Fuck you, pay me! I couldn't wait to get back home to North Carolina. I wanted to show my friends the money I made. I didn't want to go home without, being able to make more money. They say making money is like a drug. I would agree, because I was addicted. I was due to leave New York within the next week. The summer was coming to an end, so I had to be quick about things.

First, I sold all the crack I had left. Then I went to Anton's house for more. This time, I would be taking the drugs back to North

Carolina with me. Jt drove, I sat in the passenger seat, counting my money. I knew that Anton was fronting me ounces at nine hundred and fifty, so I had to get myself a better deal for five ounces. That way, I could take it down south and sell them. I knew I would have the best shit on the block. Bug would be happy. With us together, we would get this money. All I needed was Anton. As soon as we pulled up to Anton's house, we could see it was something going on. Right there in the middle of the streets, Anton was fighting with some dude. Both me and Jt, hopped out the car. I loved to fight, it's always been the one thing I knew I did well. I was right in the middle of it all. I could hear Anton talking about how dude did not have to steal from him.

Every time I came through to cop my pack, I saw this same dude there with Anton all buddy buddy, now they at each other's throats. The blows flowed with ease from Anton. He caught his target twice in the face. The friend came rushing low, which he caught Anton below the waist. He then managed to lift Anton off the ground and slammed him. He then tried to straddle Anton, but was kicked backwards. Anton got to his feet. Once he was up, he commenced to whooping dude's ass. The fight didn't last much longer after that. Anton left dude outside on the ground for all to see. He came over to us.

"What's good? Y'all ready for more already?" He was smiling at us like he had not just finished fighting. I guess money was more important than bragging about whooping his friend. Every time we came through, we spent our money, plus we had the money we owed him. It's a double good when he saw us.

"Yeah, lil cuz leaving next week, so he wants to cop something to take back with him." Jt offered.

"Damn, the summer over with already!" It wasn't a question, it was more like a statement made to himself more than to anyone in particular.

"Yeah, too damn quick!" I exclaimed, feigning anger.

"What you trying to take back with you?" He asked.

"Five ounces!" I replied.

"Now that's what's up!" Anton rubbed his hands together. You could already see him doing the math in his head. "But I'm hoping we can do it for forty five hundred, since you only hit me with the extra fifty because it was on consignment." He did not answer me, he got up, made his way to his drawer and then slid the five ounces over to me.

"Yo, that's six, just pay me before you leave." He told me, looking serious. It was a moment I would never forget because as I'm reaching for the money, I watched Anton's friend enter the room. The gun in his hand, seemed to draw all my attention like a moth to a flame. I'm sure everyone saw the gun, but I wouldn't know because my eyes were glued to the pistol. The shots rang, my mind screamed at me to run for cover, but I was struck with awe. I couldn't believe what I was seeing. The magnitude of it all was amazing. I should have been worried about being hit by a stray bullet, or a bullet aimed directly at me, but I wasn't. It was like I was the one shooting and I was liking every minute of it.

The power I felt seemed so real, I had to have it. Six quick shots! I counted them, each one. My eyes played the scene over again, the friend shot and left. Anton fell backwards and screamed out.

The girlfriend ran into the room crying and screaming. "Take this and leave!"

Then Jt grabbed me by the arm. "Let's go!" He yelled. The whole while, I could hear Anton's girlfriend crying loudly as we ran out of the house. In my hands, I still had the drugs Anton gave me. I knew then the money was still in my pocket. On the way home, Jt kept talking about how the dude was going to get his. I wasn't listening to a word he was saying, I was thinking about how easy it was to walk in, blast on a nigga and leave with all the dope and money.

"Shorty gave me the rest of the coke, Anton had!" Jt said as he saw me looking at the coke in my hands.

"I saw that!" My mind was on the nigga who came in blasting and how easy it was for him to kill. I just shook my head thinking about how Niggaz Die Every Day!

Chapter Five

* * * * *

I left New York the next week after Anton died. Before I left, Jt and I watched with amazement as the news channel flashed a young dude's face.

"I told you he was going to get his." Jt said as we looked on. Anton's killer was on all the channels. They found him in Riverhead, and he went out shooting. The shootout lasted seven minutes with the killer being the only death. Bystanders were saying how crazy it was that the police gunned down an innocent man. We, on the other hand, knew better. We knew that there was nothing innocent about dude at all. I could imagine the smile on Anton's girlfriend's face. I bet she was somewhere watching, laughing. I made it back to North Carolina with the six ounces and I couldn't wait to see my friends. My mother wanted me to spend some time with her and my little brother, Khafil, but that was short-lived as the doorbell rang. I smiled mischievously because I knew it was my boys.

My mother answered the door. " Hi, ma!" My friends could be heard greeting her.

"Hi, y'all! He's upstairs in his room!" She couldn't even be mad at them; she knew how close we were.

"What up, doe?" Benny yelled coming through my room door. We dap then shoulder hug.

"Ain't nothing! What y'all been doing while I was gone?" I was asking while I greeted the rest of my homeboys. We were all in my room. The Crew, as we liked to call ourselves.

"The same shit every day. We saw you coming down the road." Bug stated.

"Yeah, I saw y'all over there faking like y'all know how to ball…" I joked.

"Faking? Man, all y'all know I ain't no faker out there. I'm the best out here!" Leroy boasted. It's true, Leroy was the one who played ball for the school team. Him being the best was a long shot. He may be better than us, but he was far from the best out there.

"Whatever, let's see who the best round here!" I exclaimed while I tightened my sneakers up. We left my house to go down the street to ball. Once we get to the court, I start telling The Crew about my summer up top—New York, as we call it. I tell them about the money I was making up there. No one believed me. I explained how I was selling crack and the money came with ease. I even tried to express the way I watched Anton die. It was like no one was interested at all, so I stopped talking and started to ball. Two games in, I won one game of 21, while Benny and Leroy whooped me and Lil G in a two-on-two game. The next game, I played with Bug and we beat Leroy and Benny, who claimed they lost only because they were tired. I wasn't trying to hear that hot shit. I accepted my wins however I got them. While everyone was talking about one thing or another, I pulled Bug to the side. "Yo! I got a couple of ounces."

"Of what? Some weed?" Bug asked.

"Nah! Crack!" He was staring at me like I was stupid, so I continued. "I'm serious!"

"So, what you wanna do?" He asked me.

"Fuck you think! Let's get this money!" I guess it was the look in my eyes or the tone of my voice because I knew then Bug knew I was serious.

"I'm wit it!" We dapped and then shoulder hugged.

"Y'all through hugging or is it going to be more?" Benny's sarcastic ass said.

"Fuck you!" I replied.

"Well, let's get another game." Benny threw the ball at me. We played another game and of course my team lose, but that was cool to us, because we both had money on our mind. The next morning, I was up early. I had to meet Bug down by his house. We needed to get to his cousin's house so we could start getting this money. In my mind, that morning was to be this perfect start to a new beginning, but it wasn't. That morning, I woke up to find my mother crying. There was nothing I hated more than to hear my mother cry. I quickly went to her room, hoping and praying that her new boyfriend hadn't put his hands on her.

When I walked into her room, I noticed she was on the phone. It was there in that moment she looked into my eyes. I couldn't know what it was that had her feeling so sad, but her sadness caused me to swell up inside. I could see her watery eyes the closer I got to her.

"What's wrong, ma?" I wanted to know what caused her so much pain.

"It's your cousin—" She said, her voice barely above a whisper, but I understood. I knew exactly what she said.

"MY COUSIN? WHAT HAPPEN?" I already knew what she was going to say, but I held on to my ignorance for a moment longer.

"Jt died this morning. He crashed his car into a tree last night." My mother's words came out in pieces. The tears and her shaky voice made her words extra choppy. The message was too clear, though. My cousin was dead! There was nothing I could say, he was gone. I was just with him the other day and now he's gone. Through my mind's eye, I saw him smiling at me. I could hear Jt and Perry, both of them talking to me. I could see them both reaching their hands out to me. My mother was still talking to me, but I had long ago blocked out her voice. All I could hear is Jt calling my name. I could see my mother's lips moving but it wasn't her voice I heard. I was hearing Perry's voice. "Imma whoop ya ass!" I was hearing Jt's voice. "Just remember to keep that animal inside you!" I heard Anton's voice. "Might as well get some money while you here!" I was smiling, but the pain was evident in my heart.

My mother, Khafil, and I, left North Carolina to go to New York, the next day. Jt, was buried in the same cemetery as my grandmother. I hated to see his body going into the ground. I stood there paying my respects but secretly wishing I wasn't there. After the burial, we went back to my aunt's house. Everyone was downstairs eating, drinking, and talking. I was upstairs in Jt's room. I found some basketball cards that I packed up to take back home with me. Then I came across the Timberland box I knew Jt kept all his secrets in. Inside was exactly what I had expected. The money and the drugs I knew would be there, were there. I took those along with some clothes I thought I could fit back home with me.

Chapter Six

* * * * *

I left New York and returned to North Carolina a new person. My whole attitude on life switched up. I had seen too much! I was certain that death was coming for me. How was it not? It seemed to be everywhere I was or was not. This would have scarred most kids my age, but all it did was feed me the fuel to act out. I took those drugs and that money I got from Jt's room and I went extra hard on the streets. I made it a point not to bring anything into my mother's home, but she heard the stories, she knew what was going on. My school activities become more frequent, even though I wasn't in any school activities. I only would tell my mother I was doing those, just so I could do more in the street. I went from going to school every day to going to school only when needed. I no longer had any intentions on getting an education from teachers. My education was coming from the streets of Fayetteville. We only spent a month or two selling out of Benny's cousin's spot. After that, we created our own block, one closer to our side of the neighborhood. Soon, everyone was coming to us for the crack rock. Eventually, we sold out and I had to find a new plug to get the drugs. We did! We started copping from Benny's cousin then our spending habits became overwhelming. Even though we still managed to keep some work, we never had as much as we did when I first came back from New York. This is when we started robbing folks.

No one thought I would graduate from high school, but I did. I always made it to school when I had to. My grades weren't the best, but I always passed. Bug used to say the only reason we passed grade after grade was because the teachers wanted to get rid of us. That may have been true, but I didn't care, I was only happy to be moving on. Three years after Jt died, I found myself walking across the stage collecting my diploma. My mother, she was so proud of me. It was like all the wrong I did over the years were erased from her mind. I could see she held high expectations for me, but I always knew, ever since the day I saw Anton get shot, that I was going be a drug dealer.

"What we getting into tonight?" I asked The Crew.

"I'm gon fuck something tonight." Leroy stated plainly. He was the one who always had girls. The pretty boy of The Crew. He was most likely going to fuck some dude's girlfriend. That's usually what he did. He couldn't care less who's girl he's with. Most fights we got into during school was because of him fucking some chick. Or when someone came up short with our money. Lil G and Benny stuck to the robberies, which is why when we were selling drugs heavy, most people stopped coming to us because of the fact that Benny and G kept robbing those we sold to. Everybody knew we were a wild bunch of young dudes, so our money wasn't like it should have been. We were too hot to fuck with. None of the dope boys would sell to us, and then none really wanted to buy from us. We stuck to our block selling twenty-dollar bags of crack and caught a few licks as they presented themselves.

"We ain't got shit poppin! What y'all trying to do?" Lil G inquired. He was the calm one. The one who always stopped to think before he agreed to do anything we did. It's Lil G, whose instincts I trusted the most.

"We just graduated, let's go out and have some fun. It's a million parties poppin off tonight! I know we can find one to slide up in!" Benny retorted. The only one of The Crew not happy was the only member who did not graduate. Bug did two years in juvie, so he never finished school, but he never was one to rain on our parade.

"What's up with you?" I asked him.

"I'm good!" Bug shot back, but I for one was not convinced.

"Nigga, What's up? You over there looking like you lost your puppy." I was joking with him, but he really did look like he lost a puppy or something.

"Ain't lose shit, but I know one thing I ain't about to be out there partying when all this money gon be coming through! Y'all niggaz go ahead have fun just bring a bitch back for me!" Bug exclaimed as he jumped up from the seat he was glued to just minutes ago. He took his time busting down a Dutch Master cigar. I gave him some weed from my pocket to roll up. I wanted to smoke too, and the more I thought about what he had just said, the more I realized tonight would be a great night to come up on some cash. It's Friday night and all those fiends that spend cash with us were loyal.

"Fuck it! Since everybody going to be out partying. I say we set up on our block and bum rush Traps spot too. I know them fools going out tonight. Shit gon be wide open." I said this to get the whole crew to be a part of tonight's money mission. I could see them thinking and trying to weigh my words against what they knew they could get into tonight. The girls at the clubs would be out looking like super freaks.

"Talking that bum rush shit is right up my alley! I'm wit it!" Benny expressed overly loud. I could hear the wheels churning inside Lil G's head as they always do. He was weighing the pros against the cons, I bet.

"Stop that shit!" Benny waved his hands in front of G's face.

"What?" Lil G asked as if he didn't already know what.

"That thinking shit!" We all say in unison. I could only laugh out loud because I thought I was the only one who notice the wheels turning inside his head.

"Somebody gotta do it. You niggaz talking about running up in Trap's spot like he ain't the man around here!" Lil G had a point there. Trap is the man in our city, but no one was talking about running up in his spot until G mentioned it. I was only talking about setting up shop on his block, sell some rocks, and keep it moving but robbing the spot sounded like more money to us all.

"Hell yeah!" Bug shouted.

"Hey G, Boy youz a beast for real!" Leroy praised.

"What you niggaz blabbing 'bout?" G asked, sounding genuinely confused.

"We bout to run up in Trap's spot tonight."

I turned to Benny, "Hey can you get them thangs from your peoples?" Benny smiled at me. "Hell yeah!" He got up to make the call.

"Yo y'all for real? This nigga gon have some straight up goons at his spot. We ain't ready for that! We gotta plan this shit out a lot better than this dumb shit!" Lil G said trying to convince us that what we were about to do was crazy.

"Goons? Nigga, we goons!" I blurted out. " If Benny get them hammers, we up in they spot tonight!"

"You know that's a death wish!" G exclaimed.

"Hey G! Niggaz Die Every day!" I tell him just before I take a long hard pull from the blunt Bug hands to me.

Chapter Seven

* * * * *

The fiends were coming and going, so we headed to Trap's spot earlier than planned. The house, Trap used to serve his fiends was a well-known house throughout his neighborhood. Therefore, it would have been crazy for us to walk up to the door with ski mask on. Everyone outside would know what we were up to, and most likely be the reason we were found out. So, even though Lil G chose not to go with us, he gave us the sure to work plan. Bug and I were the lookout boys. I decided to take the front he took the back. Leroy and Benny were supposed to go through the front door, but nothing went as planned. When we first arrived, we took noticed to two cars parked out front the neighbors' house next to our caper. Both cars were filled with people, so we assumed they were there to cop some weed or whatever they used to party with. Benny and Leroy walked ahead of me, so I assumed they were already inside Trap's spot. I had to walk past the house and keep look out from a distance. The two cars were slightly in my way, but I could at least see the yard I was watching so I stayed put.

My eyes played tug o' war with the house and the two cars. Watching for trouble from both. The gun that was concealed within my waistline was heavy enough to consider that fact that

I had never had to use a pistol violently. I carried a gun just to scare someone enough to give up they possessions. I am mostly a fighter. In fact, I'll fight anyone, anywhere, for any reason, but a killer, I was not. I waited at least ten minutes for those two cars to leave but they never moved. I could see the occupants inside moving around like they had nowhere in particular to be. Then, I heard the gunshots, I saw both cars pull away quickly and leave the block. I ran at top speed toward the front door of Trap's crack house. I had the pistol down by my side as I ran, ready to pull the trigger. Before I got to the door, I heard more shots ring out. I was no longer thinking. I was on autopilot. I tried the doorknob. It turned and allowed me access to what was inside. The scene played out slowly, but slowness was the last thing anyone of us wanted to be.

In front of me was a couch with one guy behind it ducking from the bullets coming from the opposite direction which I thought had to be a hallway. As I was staring toward the hallway, I caught a glimpse of the man behind the couch facing me and turning his gun my way. I reacted the way I should have, and thanked God I was faster.

My gun spat bullets that ripped through the couch and found homes within the intended targets body. Even though I could plainly see he was dead, I continued to shoot in his direction because, I knew had his aim been better, I was a goner. To my left, I could still hear shots, so I turned my attention that way. I kept my back against the wall nearest the front door. I wasn't sure of what to expect around the corner and down the hall. My mind was on nothing but survival. I continued to inch my way closer to the hallway, expecting to get to a better understanding of what lies beyond. The closer I came to the corner, the more I began to focus on the body in all black. I let my gun lead the way and as I watched where I was going. I noticed my arms and the fact that I was wearing all black. The body on the floor next to me was dressed pretty much the same as me.

It dawned on me then that this body, this dead person, had to be someone from my crew. I slowly and quietly knelt down beside the body to get a better look at the person's face. His face immediately took the breath from my body. Somewhere within the time of me kneeling down to examine my friend's body the gun shots came to an end. Leroy lay dead before me and I knew somehow it had to be my fault. I was supposed to be at the front door backing him up.

"Benny!" I yelled out, not caring who heard me. I needed to know if both my friends were dead or just the one. "Mecca, that you?" I heard.

"He's dead!" I yelled back. From behind me, I heard footsteps. In my mind, I was moving quick, but the fact that Benny was already on my side kneeling down, told me I had moved too slow to stop any threat that could have been coming my way. "Damn!"

"We can't leave him here!" I whispered. From behind us, Bug came out with a trash bag in his hands.

"We can't leave him here!" I repeated.

"We can't take him with us!" Bug touched my shoulder. It was then, when I looked up at Bug, that I remembered the time when Anton's girlfriend gave us the drugs and told us to leave. Leroy, my friend, my brother, dead and gone. *Niggaz Die Every Day,* I thought. I closed his eyes just before I stood to leave.

"Grab his gun!" I said to Benny as I pulled the hoodie over my head. I knew he deserved better, but we did have to go, so I left him there on the floor and ran out the house with the rest of my crew. That night we left three bodies and only walked away with six thousand dollars and three ounces of crack. Nothing worth the life of our brother and friend, Leroy "Prettyboy" Hogue.

Chapter Eight

* * * * *

Leroy's death became a major part of the streets' gossip. What's crazy is, somehow nothing about the three bodies or the robbery attempt made the news. The police came through and wrote it off as a robbery gone bad. Most people who knew Leroy, knew he ran with The Crew. The talk about The Crew reached all the way up to Trap, who wanted nothing more than to meet these boys. He knew exactly how much money and drugs were missing from his spot. He wanted to know who these young wild niggaz were.

The word that Trap wanted to meet came by way of Benny's cousin. He supplied guns to most people in the Ville (Fayetteville), anyone who was anyone knew that Benny's cousin, Orlando, had the weaponry. Even though everyone was privy to this knowledge, Orlando did not want Trap to know anything about his involvement, as far as the guns go. He was afraid that Trap would accuse him for setting things in motion. To safeguard himself, he spoke to Benny, trying to get him to reconcile with Trap. It took 24 hours for Trap to find out exactly who robbed him. Meanwhile, the police knew nothing or either careless to find out who done what and why. That fact alone made The Crew wonder which was worst. The police or Trap?

"I don't care if he wanna talk to us or not. That dude ain't gon say it's cool y'all good. He gon pop off! Naw! Not me!" Benny expressed his thoughts on the situation.

"Yo! If dude wanted to get at us, he already know who we are. Fuck it, I say we go see what he want. If he wanna buck, then we buck!" Bug shrugged his shoulders as he spoke.

"Naw. I say we don't go anywhere. Dude wants to talk to us, he know where we at!" I voiced. The whole time we talking, Lil G was shaking his head at us. He wanted to say "I told you so!" but out of respect for Leroy, he held his tongue.

"Y'all scared, huh?" Bug stood up. He pulled back the slide on the pistol he held tightly in his clutches.

"Don't trip! Y'all stay here, I'll go meet him by myself!"

"For what?" Benny asked.

"Cause we gotta get this shit over with. We gon get along or we gon clash! Either way, life gotta go on. Y'all scared, fuck it, I understand, but I ain't letting that old ass nigga put fear in me. My gun bust just like his do!" Bug continued.

"Bug, that nigga got more shooters than we do!" Lil G tried to reason with him.

"WE!" Bug shouted.

"Yeah, WE! If you go, I'm going! I ain't letting you go by yourself!" G explained.

"Me neither!" I added.

"Fuck!" Benny said, shaking his head at us.

"Ain't that what you told Mecca? Niggaz Die Every Day!"

"Not today, fam!" I wasn't in the mood for G's smart ass remarks, so I did not give him the satisfaction of knowing how it affected me. I wasn't about to let another one of my friends die on my watch. We were all going to survive together or die in the process. On the outside, I was tough as nails, but inside—I was shitting bricks. Death has ways of finding us all, but today, hoped it wasn't any of our time to die. We spent most of the day bullshitting, but eventually we all piled up in Bug's Ford Focus and drove over to where Trap wanted to meet.

Through the whole ride over, I was checking my gun to make sure it was loaded. Lil G sat in the back with me. I could see the wheels turning in his head as usual. Up front, Bug was calm, but Benny kept messing with the radio, so Bug stopped him. Everyone was nervous, but no one would speak on it. When we arrived, Trap had two guys positioned outside the front door. Maybe to announce our arrival or may be to scare us. Both duly noted in my book of things. As we had expected, they wanted to search us, and we refused to be searched. They knew we were strapped just like we knew they were strapped. They started to get antsy and so did we. Trap had to come outside to defuse the situation, because a lot of itchy fingers and a few nervous ones could lead to everybody making tonight's news. We followed Trap inside to what I guessed would be considered the living room. There was no sign of life, but the fold out table and chairs told us this was and or could be our last time alive together.

"You four, the young wild niggaz they call The Crew?" Trap said in a tone that said he was neither mad nor happy about the robbery or the men who died that day. Not one to speak for us, I said nothing.

"I'm going to take your silence as an answer to my question. You boys killed two of my people and I also believe your friend died as well." Trap said.

Sensing that we were not going to speak, he continued on. "Judging by the way y'all strapped and how quiet you are, Imma get to the point! You took something small to me, but what you took means nothing at all. It's what you represent to the streets and all those onlookers. You wild young niggaz make people think it's okay to try me. That's something I cannot have! So, you have a choice here and now. Be a friend of mine, or become my enemy!"

Trap took this moment to judge the reactions upon the faces of those around him. Even though none of us spoke, I could tell that he knew and understood our silent answer. He asked anyway.

"So, what's it gonna be?" His voice was loud and demanding. His men stood straighter, more alert. I had to step up or there would be no telling what Bug might have said.

"Be friends!" I replied.

He nodded his head in agreement. "First things first. Since you all owe me some money, I have a job for you." He slid me an envelope, I knew just from touching it there was money inside. I looked from Trap to the envelope and back at Trap again. He smiled at me. I decided then I didn't like his smile. It was untrustworthy.

"That's your payment. It would have been more, but like I said, you niggaz owe me!"

"What's the job?" Bug asked first.

"Simple! You little muthafuckas work for me now! You stay on that shitty little block of yours until I say otherwise. I'll supply the work, you fools pay on time. If the time arises, and I need some little shitheads to put in work, I'll give you wild niggaz a call." Trap told us.

"And if we refuse?" Lil G wanted to know. The answer came by the way of shotguns, pistols, and automatic rifles being cocked back. The sound alone took my breath away. The few men Trap had standing by seemed to have tripled in that moment. Trap stood there amongst his people smiling at us with that devilish smile of his. I disliked his smile even more. He was looking like a proud father did when watching his son hit the winning home run at a baseball game.

"Again! Your choice!" *Our choice*, I thought to myself. Our choice! Sure! I passed the money off to Lil G.

"Trust me, we underdig!" I wanted to say fuck you, but I knew there was no way we would leave there alive. "I'll send someone round there with the work later on." Trap assured us. I turned my back to him, but I could feel them staring at us so hard that I turned back towards them walking out backwards while watching them watching us.

"We about to come up big!" Bug was excited.

"He just SONNED us!" Benny said through gritted teeth.

"We alive, ain't we?" I tried to remind everyone of this fact. "We rich!" Bug was excited.

"Rich?" Lil G questioned.

"Yeah! Once he starts hitting us with the work, we gon---"

"Owe him!" Lil G finished Bug's statement with his own.

"That's not what I wanted to say but yeah we pay him keep the rest." Bug confirmed.

"Naw, we gon play along for now, but I ain't liking this shit. A month from now, we gon rob this pussy nigga dry!" G blurted. We all looked at G. We couldn't believe it was him who was saying this.

"Don't trip bout it! I got this one!" G responded to our stares.

"You must have a plan!" I assume.

"I do!" He told us.

"What's on your mind?" Benny wanted to know. We were all ears. " Remember when you said, Niggaz Die Every Day?"

Chapter Nine

* * * * *

The women were in abundance and Trap was happy to be amongst the men in the club tonight. There were not too many places Trap considered himself comfortable at, but he always was able to let his guard down when he came to Heaven on Earth. The strip club being owned by a friend of his, made everything that much more relaxing. The girls were sexy, and the people were so respectful, one couldn't help but to come back for more. The best part about coming to Heaven on Earth was the fact that he could get a piece of pussy from whichever female that fit his fancy. There were so many to choose from, Trap could only wait to see who he'd wind up with. There were special rooms for those who could afford them, which is why Trap spent his time in such rooms whenever he came. Around Heaven on Earth, money did the talking and Trap had plenty of money.

"I see you are enjoying yourself!" Black said as he walked inside Trap's private room.

"I always do! Where's the man himself or did you travel alone this time?" Trap asked, speaking of the owner who was never in the club.

"He around here somewhere. You know he has so much to do, check this bitch, that bitch, he here though!" Black's eyes fell on the bookbag that was seated next to Trap. This was somewhat their regular routine. Trap pushed the bookbag towards Black who looked inside to confirm that it was all cash.

"Business seems well!" He noted.

"That's the one thing I do best!" Trap said proudly.

"Well, keep doing what you doing! If you want to step ya game up, just come see me!" Black stood up to leave.

"I been thinking about that, I just have to send someone up your way. I could save you the trip and me some money!" Trap was searching for Black's approval. The drive to Virginia would save him four thousand a key of cocaine and the weed would drop from three thousand a pound to twenty five hundred. All in all, Trap could save himself twenty five grand a week. Within a month, he could double his regular purchase. To him it was well worth the risk of the drive.

"That's what up! Just know when that shit leaves us, it's yours! Know yo people!" Black knew best how easy it was to be tempted when money was involved. Trap spent close to one hundred and fifty grand every week, sometimes more. That kind of money will make close friends change sides.

"I'm on it! I rather we make this a once a month thing." Trap said.

"We can do that, but understand when it comes to my paper... friends, family, wives, girlfriends, grandmas, mommas, all of 'em can get it." Black was laughing, but Trap knew how serious he was. Black's reputation preceded him.

"Imma put some more money together and come up that way. I say we do the month thing." Trap ignored the slight threatening comment and continued to discuss business. A beautiful Spanish girl walked into the room, causing both men to look up at her.

"Sorry, I didn't mean to interrupt. Chrome said I should come up here." The sexy Spanish girl explained.

"No need to be sorry, ma. I was just leaving." Black says smiling at the girl. "Enjoy yourself!" He told Trap.

"I always do!" Before the door was completely closed, Black could hear the female laughing. He smiled thinking how well his cousin, Chrome knew how to entertain his guests.

Coming through the doors of Heaven on Earth, was like walking into a room full of pussy. Actually, that's exactly what it was. Me and Bug made it our business to come through any time one of the strippers felt the need to buy some coke. With so many drug dealers around, the girls usually had their favorites. Being that my crew was known for unsportsmanlike conduct, we usually were the last choice. I never let that bother me none, either way... we made our money. Most of the customers were military guys. They snorted more coke than the civilians. That night, my eyes fell on the pimp I saw there every now and then. He from New York, I only knew this because these females talk too damn much and I'm halfway nosy. It wasn't him that caught my attention, it was the big dude next to him with the bookbag that had all my attention.

My first thought was to wait outside to see exactly what that bookbag held. I had to have been staring too hard because for some reason the Pimp looked me dead in the eyes. I nodded my head, he held up his drink, and then we both went back to what we were doing. Me, I pretended to be talking to Bug, but really, I was still watching dude with the bookbag.

"Yo!" Bug tapped me. I was so stuck in my thoughts that I didn't notice Bug trying to get my attention. When I did acknowledge him, he was standing with Trap. Both of these fools were smiling!

"What's good?" I say extending my hand out to Trap.

"He was just telling me he wants us to go up VA." Bug was talking, I was nodding my head, but I was looking back, and I noticed the Pimp was gone, but the big guy with the bookbag was coming my way. Our eyes met once again, but this time, I could see that this dude was either drunk as hell or the fire red in his eyes meant trouble. I broke eye contact to acknowledge Bug and Trap.

"VA? What's up. there?" I was talking to them, but the bookbag guy answered.

"Everything!"

"Black, these the little niggaz Imma send up there to see you." Trap introduced us. My instincts and curiosity were at an all-time high. I knew this dude was somebody important, but who?

"Tru indeed! Y'all enjoy yourselves while you here. I'll see you when you come up my way." His tone was neutral, but I could tell he trying to dismiss us.

"Aight, y'all let the grown folks talk." Trap waved us off. It was taking everything in me not to slap Trap's bitch ass. It was Bug's dumb ass all "Yes, sir" and shit. I walked off without saying a word.

Fuck them fools, I thought. I found me a bad little black girl to press up on. Whole time I'm with her, I'm watching Trap and Black talk. After a while, the Pimp came over to them, and whatever he said had them all laughing hard. I got tired watching them, so I let the little sexy chick who was in front of me, do her dance thing on my lap. I fed her some coke and before while she was explaining to me that the Pimp, his name was Chrome, and the dude with the bookbag, Black, he was the man with that work. She kept talking, but all I was hearing was that he was the man with that work! I found Trap's connect.

Chapter Ten

* * * *

"This nigga ain't say dude had this many bitches! Man, look at that bitch right there!" Benny exclaimed. "I see her!" Lil G said calmly.

"Nigga I would beat dat pussy so bad, she would have to file charges out on me." Benny continued.

"It's a good thing we out here to watch that nigga and not them bitches. So, focus on him."

"Trust me, I see him. He ain't going nowhere without them hoes. Nigga, that red bone could get every dollar in my pockets, right now!" Benny said looking over at Lil G. They were parked outside the club Heaven on Earth, waiting for the Pimp to come out. Mecca called them to keep an eye out for Chrome.

He was convinced that the Pimp would be an easy lick. What started out to be a few hours ended up being all night. It was like the Pimp had to stay all night to watch his girls make money. Mecca and Bug kept tabs on the Pimp while he was inside the club. Once he left, it was up to Benny and Lil G to follow the Pimp home and then call the rest of The Crew over. The plan was to take the Pimp and his hoes for everything they had.

"From what Mecca said, all them hoes got plenty of money tonight. So, I'm guessing that dude got a few thousand on him right now." G noted.

"He better have more than a few thousand." Benny replied now looking at G.

"Why you think we following him home? This nigga got to have more cash at home. Them bitches work every night, I bet!" In his brain, G already calculated they could come off close to fifty grand. Completely aware of Mecca and Bug's eyes watching him all night, Chrome made sure to stay at the club a lot longer than he usually would. He wanted to see how determined the two young boys were willing to go. From the looks of things, they were willing to go the extra mile. They spent the whole night at the club, from what Chrome assumed they could catch him alone. He smiled at the thought of these two or anyone trying to rob him. He thought about how he told Black to go ahead and leave without him. He wasn't too worried about them doing him much harm. He knew from Trap that they both were easy to be touched since they work for him.

To his surprise, he watched them leave before him. He began to think that maybe he was becoming paranoid. It was possible that the people who saw him could see the money he represented. They may not have known him, but anyone could see that he was worth lots of dough. Mostly, he would travel with The Baldhead Murderer, but sometimes his pride wouldn't allow him to travel with protection. He liked to travel with his girls, alone. The only protection he needed was the .45 he carried with him. To say Chrome was a killer would be wrong but, would he kill? Yes! Would he care if he killed someone tonight? No! Across the parking lot, Benny and Lil G sat in their car watching Chrome, who just came out the club with four girls in tow. They all got into a dark blue Range Rover and drove down Bragg Boulevard. Benny followed close behind, but not too close that he could have been recognized.

They drove down Bragg, onto Skibo Road where they waited for the light to turn green, so they could go to The Fairfield Inn. Benny kept straight at the light, not even turning his head in the direction of the Range Rover. He and Lil G, both knew it would be too much of a coincidence if they were going to the same hotel. He drove down Skibo until he passed two lights and then he quickly made the U-turn. Pulling into the parking lot of The Fairfield Inn, they could see that the Pimp and his hoes were already inside. They found a spot to park a few spaces down from the Range Rover.

"We going in?" Benny asked.

"Nah, we wait!" Lil G answered.

"For what?" He asked.

"They only here visiting, once they take their showers, smoke, fuck, whatever they do. We go in there and wake they ass up with guns in they faces."

Funny as life is, Chrome had always been the type of dude who believes in life's unexpected moments. From the window in his room, he watched as the same car that followed him out the club, pulled into the parking lot and park a few spaces down from his truck. That smile of his came back, but it was fueled by rage.

His first thought was to call Trap and see if he had his hand in this spectacle, but he dismissed the thought. Instead, he left the window and made his way down to the front desk. The clerk was a woman, Chrome made a special point in getting to know. Not only was it important for his business, it was also important for him. He needed to know that if and or when the police came rushing the hotel looking for him or his girls, he wanted to be sure at least the front desk clerk would alert him of the threat. The closer he got to the front desk, the bigger the smile spread across the clerk's face.

"I got some people coming through in a few. Could you be a dear and direct them to my room?" The smile he smiled for her is a smile that melts many of women, young and old.

"Sure thing, Mr. Jones!"

"I told you before, cuteness, call me Chrome." She smiled bashfully, as she stared at his back, wondering all the things there was to wonder about a pimp.

* * * * *

I was sitting in the car with Bug when Trap called my phone. It wasn't the call I had been expecting, but one I was expected to answer. The first thing out Trap's mouth, "Do you remember the dude I introduced you to tonight?"

Of course, I remembered him, he was the connect. I felt a sensation creeping through my body. I was waiting for G to call me with the Pimp's whereabouts and here was Trap wanting to talk about the bookbag guy.

"Yeah, I remember, what's good?" I was hoping this wasn't going to be a long drawn out conversation. It was getting late. I just wanted to get this money and catch some much-needed sleep.

"Good I just got off the phone with him. Imma need two of you to go to VA with me and two of youz to ride with his cousin down south." Trap said.

"His cousin?"

"Yeah I'll introduce y'all in the morning but, I'm sure you saw him at the club. Cool cat, long dreads, real pimp type nigga!" The words pimp, hit me like a ton of bricks. I knew right then that if I didn't get off the phone with Trap and call Lil G that shit was going to get real and fast. I had to hurry this call along. I started waving my hands frantically trying to get Bug's attention. He just got out the car to speak to a girl who was walking across the parking lot at IHOP.

"Yeah, I seen him."

"I'm sure you did! Any who, be here in the morning." Trap ordered.

"What time?"

"In da morning, nigga!" Trap yelled I could have played this game with him over and over, but I needed to make a call. So instead, I simply said. "Bet dat up!"

As soon as I ended the call, I was calling G.

"What's good, fam?" G answered.

"Yo! Abort mission. ASAP!" I told him.

"Why, we here now!" G retorted.

"My nigga, Abort mission! I'll explain everything when you get here!"

"Where you at?" He asked.

"Meet us at the crib!" Bug's black ass finally got back in the car when I ended the call with G.

"Why, you waving at me all crazy like? You seen that bitch, huh?" Bug slid into the driver's seat, asking.

"Because, nigga! Trap just called and he wants us to ride to VA in the morning."

"We already knew that, so!" Bug replied.

"Guess what the fuck we ain't know!"

"What?" Bug asked.

"The Pimp nigga some kin to the connect!"

"Oh word?" Bug replied, impressed.

"Yeah, and we was about to rob his ass!" I told him.

"About to? I thought we are!" Bug blurted out.

"Nigga you ain't hearing shit I'm saying is you? The Pimp is the dude Black's cousin! Trap wants us to ride with the Pimp in the morning down south. If we rob the damn dude, we gon have more trouble than just Trap ass."

"Damn! That nigga must have an horseshoe up his ass!" Bug replied.

"We the lucky ones! Trap just saved our lives and he don't even know it!"

"Whatever yo! Them niggaz bleed just like we do!" Bug replied.

I'm glad I was the one Trap called because if it had been Bug, I'm sure he would have let Lil G and Benny bum rush the Pimp. I had to shake my head at this dude. He just doesn't understand how life works. He thinks it's all fun and games, get money, and show people how tough he is. He does not think about the people in the world who think exactly like he do. The ones who happen to be tougher, quicker, smarter, and a lot more dangerous than he. Death is waiting around the corner for us all, I for one am not in a rush to meet her. Bug on the other hand seems to think he's untouchable like death has no claim to him. I know a mistake when I see one, and touching that pimp nigga was about to be a big mistake.

From his window, Chrome watched the car leave the hotel. He still felt rage inside himself, but thought it was funny how life could be. Walking away from the window, he tossed the gun he held on the bed. He then made a call to Rachel, the Spanish girl he had with him. She was in a room two doors down from his own. When she answered he told her to leave her room and to

63

come to his. He also explained to her to bring some blunts. He no longer had any and he knew for sure that she did. She arrived quickly, softly knocking on the door which was already open for her to enter. Chrome took one look at her robe and he knew underneath she had nothing but skin. The high heels she wore were red, and the way she wore them was enough to make many of men want her even more. To Chrome, she was a money maker but, in that moment, she was to be his stress reliever. She passed him the blunts he asked for, which he used to roll up some weed. Once he had the weed smoke flowing through out the air, she placed her head in his lap. She fondled him just enough to arouse her favorite man tool. Once her tool was nice and hard, she took it upon herself to release it from its captivity. Once freedom was real, she surrounded her lips around his tool causing, Chrome's head to lean back in pleasure. The weed, along with the intense sexual comfort, that Chrome endured, displayed the successful outlook on life he felt. To him all things came in due time. All he had to do was wait and everything in life he ever wanted would come to him.

He had seen many people fall from success and he has seen many people fall from too much comfort. What he valued most was knowledge and he knew then that there had to be something done to those who thought that he was a victim. Even though his body was in pure bliss, his mind continued to think and replay the actions of those young boys. Something had caused them to stop what they obviously had in motion.

"I'm going to nip that shit in the bud!" He moaned softly to himself, causing Rachel to look up at him, hoping she hadn't just done something he didn't like.

Chapter Eleven

* * * * *

T he next morning, I left the house before my mother was able to wake my brother for school. I had to walk down to Benny's house, wait for him to get dressed, and then together we strolled down to Bug's house. Lil G was already with Bug when we arrived, so we all piled inside Benny's car and left. The four of us being together in one car made me realize how much I missed, Leroy. Thinking of him brought back memories of Jt and Perry. All three of them were like brothers to me. Now they were gone, and I could not let their memory be a sad one. I didn't have to make myself smile as I thought about Jt's fast ass junk car. Nor did I have to fake a smile when I thought about the time me and Perry, fought them dudes in the alleyway. I missed them both! I remembered one time, Leroy was fucking this girl. Me and Benny was outside the house waiting for him to come out. The girl's boyfriend showed up. He saw us in the car alongside the curb. We were parked in front of the house, so he knew what time it was. He watched us, so we watched him.

Meanwhile, Leroy was in the house deep inside his girlfriend. Soon, the door opened, and Leroy came out the house. Same time, dude was walking up to the door. They got into a brief argument, but before me and Benny could get to them, Leroy was smacking the dude with both hands. Left, right, left, right, back and forth. The shit was so funny cause dude just stood there while Leroy continued to assault his face over and over. Dude's head went side to side with each slap. What made matters worse was how fast Leroy was slapping him. I laughed so hard, that if dude had tried to fight back, I would have been no help 'cause I was damn near on the ground in tears. I remember laughing so much my cheeks hurt. Damn! I miss my dog! The smell of weed brought me back to today, the moment at hand.

We arrived at Trap's house, some dude I never saw before was directing us where to park. Lil G had just given me the blunt, but from how hard I was pulling on it, you would have thought I had smoked it by myself. Yeah, I was nervous but why, I didn't know, call it a gut feeling. The front yard was filled with all Trap's goons. They stood in front of a black truck with chrome rims. I seen the truck before, so I knew it belonged to a cat named Cedric. Cedric is one crooked ass cop, but he young and cool as hell and from our hood. Still, he the police. Trap came out the front door with Cedric and The Pimp Nigga. I then noticed the Range Rover next to Cedric's truck, both of them were fly as hell. The vehicles, of course! The trio walked out like they were the best of friends. It was enough to make me wanna puke. Truth is I don't like Trap, I ain't got shit bad to say bout Cedric or the pimp nigga but all three of them got something I want and I wished like hell I could take it from them. One day I will. Right now, we just playing nice. Trap finally realized we were there, he whispered something to the cop and without a response Cedric left. Once Cedric was gone, Trap and The Pimp made their way over to us.

"This is Chrome, and these the wild ass young niggaz I've been telling you about." Trap said as way of introduction. I could have sworn I saw a hint of recognition in Chrome's eyes. I thought to myself maybe he had spotted us last night, but I knew he didn't. These niggaz would be beefing with us instead of smiling at us.

"Young wild niggaz, huh? Have these two ride with me and send the others up to Black. I'll send them back in a U-Haul with the greenery!" Chrome's voice was smooth like a pimp's voice should be. Lil G and Benny, both looked at me. I knew they were thinking the same thing I was. This Pimp nigga know what's up! Trap must think we some fools. Yeah, we young, but we far from dumb.

"Naw. We don't rock like that we all stay together. I ain't going nowhere with this dude. I don't know him!" Benny spoke up.

"Young wild and scary too!" Chrome said stepping up to Benny.

"I ain't never scared!" Benny voiced proudly, not backing down from Chrome.

"Then take your bone crushing ass to that truck with them Bitches! You riding with me!" Chrome's voice was one of authority, someone who was not used to anyone challenging him.

"Don't trip, fam! You and G ride wit dude—"

"Chrome! My name is Chrome! Look, what's up with you niggaz?"

"Look no disrespect! We just don't know you, so you have to excuse us if we not so trusting about jumping in your ride to head out of town with you!" Lil G explained.

"You little niggaz don't need to trust me and frankly I don't give a fuck! I'm riding with a bunch of bitches so if you niggaz worried about some hoes, then grow the fuck up." Chrome spat out.

"All you niggaz need to worry bout is making sure my shit get back here safe." Trap seethed. He was looking at us like he was mad at the world. I ain't care, fuck him too!

"Whatever yo! We got this! Y'all go head do dat shit, we gon handle up top." Bug says to us interrupting the cold stare Trap was giving us.

"Smart man!" One of Trap's men stated. We all turned around to see who it was who thought we were suckers.

"What, that pistol supposed to mean something to me?" Bug asked him.

"Let it go!" Chrome demanded. "We got money to make, let's go!" He smiles turning away from us and everyone outside. The way he spoke was like he was the boss of Trap's men. I watched my friends climb inside the Range with Chrome. Lil G took the front, Benny got in the back with The Pimp. They left first, we then left as well, taking 95 North, my favorite highway to Virginia!

Chapter Twelve

* * * * *

It took us four hours to get to VA, and when we got there, we spent the next two hours driving to some town called Manassas. Once we were at the place to be, we met up with Black and his bald head friend. They already had a U-Haul truck loaded for us to drive back. Trap was supposed to follow us back, which was the plan on the way up, but I quickly learned that us driving back was not the only thing they had in mind for us. Maybe it was the way the bald dude kept watching us, or maybe it was how Black and Trap kept whispering to each other and looking our way. Either or, I knew something wasn't right. I had to wait until we were alone to express my thoughts to Bug. That opportunity never came. I remember thinking everything was all a joke, but the eyes never lie and the way the bald head dude was peering into my soul, told me we were in deep shit. Benny sat in the back with Chrome, talking about pimpin, the whole drive. The girls in the back with them, were laughing and cooing about whatever. Lil G sat up front paying attention to everything that was going on around him.

First thing he noticed that was out of place, was the fact that they were traveling south on 95, when he knew Charlotte was west. He asked the girl who was driving, where they were going. "Ask

Daddy!" She said. Even when G did ask Chrome, told him to sit back and enjoy the ride. Never had he been one to go into anything blindly, Lil G began to protest. It was then, Chrome explained to him that it was best for him not to talk about all that he do. The fact that they were all in the car together going to the same place, showed that once they got where they were going everything will explain itself. Only thing that needed to be said was, they were going to his warehouse so they could drive back some weed for Trap.

For the rest of the trip, G said nothing. He could hear Benny in the back entertaining himself with one of the girls. He just shook his head and tried to stay on point as much as he could.

* * * * *

"What the fuck is this?" I asked, trying to stay calm. Trap had left us with Black and his bald head friend. They took the U-Haul and left. We were supposed to drive the van back, but before we got into the van, Black called us and we turned around to, two .45's pointed directly at us.

"Look, nigga, don't act surprised! You tried to rob my cousin, now this is what we do when we feel disrespected." I knew it! I fucking knew it! I should have listened to my gut. I knew shit was all wrong. I just stared at Black like he was dumb, but my mind was working a plan to escape this madness.

"I don't care who dies today but one of you niggaz die. The other, can go fuck himself for all I care." Black spat on the ground.

"Fuck you mean? Ain't no body do shit! We let that nigga make it!" Bug spat back.

"You let him make it?" Black pointed to Bug.

"Pussy! You could never let one of us make it! Matta fact, Fuck all dis talking shit! Baldhead, do what you do, with this pussy! Make sure this fuckboy dies slow!" Quickly, he swung his pistol down on Bug's head. The blow knocked Bug to the floor. I flinched, because I was about to help him out, but the vicious pain I felt creeping throughout my body caused me to fall backwards. After that, the only thing I remembered was Bug being dragged away from me, and everything around me going black.

The drive wasn't as long as G expected. They arrived at the warehouse, somewhere in Florence, SC. Inside they walked around a bit, as if Chrome was giving a tour, but he did not seem to be saying anything or pointing anything out. So, this made G think that they were heading to a certain part of the warehouse. Eventually, they came across three Spanish men who looked nothing like warehouse workers. They looked more like they were trained killers than anything else. Lil G turned to get an impression or thought from Benny, but Benny was no longer behind him. In front of him, the three guys were looking at him. Beside him, Chrome was staring daggers into him. It didn't take a rocket scientist to realize that this was a trap. His only option was to run! With nowhere to run to but the way he came, he took two, three, four steps and on the fifth step, he felt a burning sensation coming from his leg up. There was nowhere he could go, so he turned to face his attackers. All three Spanish men were there close to him, almost surrounding him. He saw Chrome smile and he wondered where Benny was.

"You little niggaz must not have known that, I don't like to be followed." Lil G said nothing, he only was thinking about the best way to escape. Even in the face of death, G had the wheels turning inside his head.

"See, this morning I told Trap about you niggaz sitting outside my hotel room and he wanted to kill you then. But me, I thought it would be better to let you niggaz understand the nature of the beast you chose to fuck with." Still, G said nothing, so Chrome continued.

"It's little niggaz like you four, that makes what we do so hard. If we black men learned how to join forces and grow together, we would probably do much better. We can't because little dumb niggaz like you rather rob the next black man and take everything he worked hard for. How come you fools don't rob a bank? Steal from them white folks? Too much of a risk, huh?"

Lil G remained silent he used his middle finger to express his feelings for Chrome. "I understand!" Chrome nodded and walked away from G, his back now to G's body.

"Just know, I only look like this, but the kid has never been a sucker!" Chrome yelled over his shoulder. Two Spanish men aimed and shot Lil G face first, leaving his body riddled with hot slugs from head to toe.

"What the fuck was that?" Benny had to push the girl off of him with both hands. Even though he was naked inside an office room, he knew that those gun shots were nothing good. He got dressed. "If something happened to my man, Imma come back up here and fuck you up, bitch!"

Out the room and down the stairs he went. At the bottom, he saw Lil G's body being dragged away by two Spanish men. He asked no questions, he simply rushed at them. He was stopped dead in his tracks when the gun one held was brandished. Then, from behind he was hit with another gun. The butt from the gun caused him to form and instant headache. From the ground, he asked Chrome. "What happen?"

"He's dead!" Chrome shrugged his shoulders like what else was there to say. Benny tried to get to his feet, but he was knocked back down.

"You lucky I'm letting you leave here alive. This shit goes against everything I believe but I do need you to take this shit to Trap and I'm sure once you get there, he will kill you himself. Even if he don't and you decide to run off with the truck... Remember we know where your family stay, so be very aware of who's life you playing with!" Chrome smiled and then he walked away from Benny.

Just as they did before, two men aimed and just before they pulled the trigger one of them asked. "Do you want this one to live?" The Spanish accent was heavy.

"Yeah! I need him to drive the truck back to Fayetteville. The keys are in the truck, but before you send him off.... Teach him a lesson or two!" Chrome laughed slightly. "Next time you think about some pussy... think about the time you tried to rob a pimp!" He told Benny.

Chapter Thirteen

* * * * *

After a brief beat down, I woke up in a car with two other people. As my eyes began to adjust, I realized I was with Black's people. I knew the driver because he delivered a few kicks to my face. A sudden urge to attack him came over me, but one look in the back seat and the gun held by another goon made me halt that decision. Noticing I was up, the driver continued to talk about me as if I wasn't there. He kept looking at me as he drove, but his words were to the guy in the back. He said something about the bald head dude being a sick muthafucka. They were laughing about how this dude liked to take his time with the people he kills. They talked about this dude like he was some type of legend. I thought he was more like a dead man, all of them were, they just didn't know it yet. I knew once I got the chance to talk to Lil G and Benny, we were going to come back and kill them all. Trap too!

First, I had to get away from these two fools. I wonder where they are taking me! I stared more deeply at my surroundings and I knew I was on the highway, but the direction was a blur.

"Where you taking me?" I asked hoping to get a straight answer.

"To Hell!" He was smiling at me but for some reason I believed I was going exactly where he said... Hell!

The whole drive back to Fayetteville seemed to be longer than the ride Benny first took. He drove half in silence, half in rage, mostly yelling to himself but at times, yelling at the other cars on the road. His mind was deeply on revenge and he could not wait to get back to Fayetteville. Chrome's men took his cellphone, so he couldn't call his friends, but once he told them what happened, he knew he would get the revenge he so desperately seeks. Hours later, he was back in Fayetteville. He did not dare go straight to Trap's place. He drove to his mother's house, in which he called Mecca. Receiving no answer, he decided to call Bug next. Again, no answer. That was when he realized that they all had been set up and his friends may be dead as well. The feeling of being in this alone made his stomach queasy. The one thing he knew for sure was that he could not bring Trap the truck and expect to live afterwards. He had to devise a plan and stall Trap out.

Actually, he decided that the truck was his plan. He removed all the weed from the truck and stored it all in his room at his mother's house. Then he called his cousin to meet him at the mall, where he planned to abandon the truck. From there, his plan consisted of him calling Trap, demanding cash for the contents he took from the U-Haul. His hope was to draw Trap out so that he could get his revenge, take the money and the weed, and then split town. Again, he had to borrow a gun from his cousin, Orlando. After Orlando left, Benny waited until it was dark outside before he made the call to Trap. He was nervous but it had to be done this way, otherwise he'll be dead before morning. The call was made, and he felt good about his plan. He was just about to get up from his bed when Mecca came through his door, looking like he had been dragged by a car.

"What the fuck happen to you?" Benny hurried to his friend.

"I'm good! They killed Bug!" He said. "G too!"

"Damn!" I said trying hard not to shed any tears. Two more friends gone before they were old enough to legally drink. "Trap and that pimp set us up!"

"No doubt! That's why we gon kill both them niggaz!" Benny showed me the gun he had tucked.

"I need one too!" Benny took the time to explain what his plan was. While he spoke, he mentioned the warehouse he got the weed from. The whole time I'm listening to him speak I was wondering what else he knew about the warehouse he went to. Since, the B&E, is how Benny usually got down he expressed in detail what he remembered seeing at the warehouse. The more he talked, the more excited I became. I was playing with the gun he just got from Orlando when it all came to me. "Let's rob they ass!"

"You think it's a stash spot?" Benny asked me.

"Hell yeah! You said it yourself, the place was full of weed and you saw the cash with your own eyes! Right?" I knew how sometimes my homeboy could add shit when he was really wanting to do something.

"Yeah, the cash was on the table next to the safe!" I said.

"Okay, then! It sounds legit to me!"

"What you wanna do?" He asked me but I knew he knew exactly what I wanted to do.

"Let's bum rush the whole thing!" That's how I felt, but I needed to know, so I asked.

"How big is it?" These types of questions were what G asked, answered, and checked so well, I knew I had to.

"Big!" was his answer. I looked at him like he was a small child who just said something dumb. "Come on! You worked with G on this type of shit for years now. He had to rub some common sense into you. They must have some type of security set up?"

"Yeah! They got all the bells and whistles but what matters most is, a bunch of Mexicans." Benny told me.

"Mexicans?"

"Yeah! A bunch of gun-toting Mexicans. They the ones who killed G, then they took turns whooping my ass." Benny had his head down. I wasn't sure of what he was thinking but it looked to me that he was really hurting.

"We gon get them back! First, we hit 'em where it hurts... them pockets! Then we come back here and knock life out that bitch ass nigga Trap!"

Chapter Fourteen

* * * * *

T he meeting Benny had set up with Trap came and went. They skipped the meeting and decided to head straight for the warehouse. It was four in the morning when they arrived, which was perfect for them. No one would be there at that hour, so they were able to get a look around. They waited an hour before they got out to get a closer look. For all intents and purposes, the building and warehouse appeared to be nothing more than a place of business. We knew better, though! It wasn't exactly what I thought it was. I was expecting, big bad ass Mexicans standing out front with big guns, ready to kill. This place was as regular as being at Home Depot or someplace else. There was no security guards or someone driving around the premises. I was beginning to think we either had the wrong place or Benny was losing it!

We walked around the building, checking windows and doors. The alarm system was obviously in place, so we didn't even try to break in. I just wanted to get a look inside. From the windows, I learned two things; one, there's no way to see inside the actual warehouse, just the lobby area. Two, there was no one inside patrolling around. When they were absolutely sure no one was inside the building they went back to the car. The time was 6:15

am. We took turns watching the building. The watching part was easy, but the sleeping was pointless being that neither one of us were sleepy.

Around 9:00 am, someone finally pulls into the lot. We could see that the person was alone which to them was a great thing. This was the moment, it was like a sign from above. Both of us, were ready, the adrenaline pumping hard through our veins. We had to wait for the guy to exit his car and when he did, we were out of our car and on his ass.

"Hurry up with that door!" Benny demanded. First thing I noticed was this man was not of Spanish descent.

"I think you fellows are mistaking me for someone else. I have no money on my person. This is simply a lumber warehouse, so you won't be finding any cash here." He pleaded, but it was cut short when the gun butt across the head made his hands push the key into the door and unlock it without any more lip.

"The alarm, hurry up!" I shouted at him, not wanting the alarm to go off because dude thought we didn't know of it. He made his way over to the alarm pad and punched in the code without speaking. The red light went green.

"I don't--" but his words again were cut short by Benny who viciously hit the man upside his head with a pistol. This caused the man to move no more. Benny then dragged his body from the lobby to the warehouse. "These crates got the weed in them. Imma go upstairs get the cash!"

"Wait! What the fuck we gon put these crates in?" We drove a small four door car with an even small trunk to match. We didn't have enough room to take shit.

"Damn, I didn't think about that! G would--" He stopped talking as he thought of our friend and brother, G.

"I know, but we ain't got much time we gotta do something."

"Fuck it! Check his pockets for his keys we just gon have to take his car too." Benny said.

"Bet!" I ran through dude's pockets found his keys, snatched them up and ran back outside. I pulled our car over first, parked it next to his and then ran back inside the warehouse. I was out of breath, but that didn't stop me. I then opened the bay door, and then from there, I emptied out crate after crate.

"The money is in the safe." Benny stated.

"Fuck it, let's bust these crates open! Look at all this weed!" I'm excited, this had to be the best lick we had ever came across. It was just so much weed! Then everything went sour. It came to us in the form of cocaine bricks. It's one thing to steal from a man. No one likes to be the one who gets robbed. Weed, it's a small thing when you think about it... but coke, there's nothing small about it. Not only did these crates have weed and coke, but after a while, we were finding crates with cash in them as well. I knew then we were in too deep.

"This ain't just weed! This coke, money and weed!"

"Load that shit!" Benny shouted. I thought back to when dude told me I was going to Hell, he wasn't far from telling the truth.

The weed game is fun, but when someone has this much coke, there is nothing to be said that makes this fun. This shit right here was life and death. I knew then that if Chrome wanted us dead before, he would really want us dead now. The Mexicans! Benny said something about Mexicans being here the last time he came. If this place had anything to do with the cartels, we are in way too deep. We had to go and go now!

"Let's get out of here!" I shouted.

"One more crate!" Benny yelled back. The moment I got my next create open, we both heard a car door slam. I looked up, Benny looked up. Both of us scanning the parking lot for whoever it was that just arrived. We saw no other car in the lot or anywhere around us, but there was no doubt in either one of our minds, we heard a door slam. My gun was in my hand ready to spit. I kept it out in front of me, just in case. I walked slowly over to the front side of our car, checking inside each window as I go along.

Just then, I heard the doors lock from the car next to ours. Inside, the man sat trying—I guess, to keep us from stealing his car. He must have thought the keys were inside, but they were not. I hit the unlock button on the keypad and the sound of the doors unlocking was heard. From inside the man locked the doors again. I unlocked them once more and then he locked them again. I unlocked them again and he did it again. I took a deep breath and tapped the window with my gun.

"If you lock these doors again, I'm going to shoot you through the window." I yelled. I unlocked the door once again, but this time, the doors stayed unlocked. I opened the door, pulled the man out, and then dragged his big ass back into the warehouse.

"Let's go!" I said to Benny as he was trying hard to stuff more drugs and money into the trunk.

"Let's go!" I repeated. Benny finally looked up at me, then over at the man. He raised his pistol and then, without any hesitation, he shot the man. Twice!

"That's for Lil G!" he said running off. I watched him rush off thinking to myself this shit is real! Nothing about this was a dream! This is real life, right now!

"Let's go!" Benny yelled out to me. I ran over to dude's car, threw Benny the keys to his car and then we both pulled out the lot. On the highway, I checked my watch. The time was 9:35 am!

Chapter Fifteen

* * * * *

I kept my eyes on the road, but I was staring at every car behind me. We just pulled off the best lick ever in our lives, but I knew it may have been the worst mistake ever. We made it back in town without any hiccups. We first dropped everything off at Benny's house. Then we took both cars to the mall, but we left the stolen car and drove away in Benny's. We were both happy about the heist. Each of us telling the story from how we saw it. Neither one of us could wait to get back and count the profits.

"Damn, I wish the boys were here to see this shit." Benny's voice was at a whisper, not wanting his mother to hear us. Everything we stole was on the floor and bed inside Benny's small bedroom. We were so in a rush that we never took the time to hide anything. It's a good thing Benny's mom never came into his room. "They can see us!"

It took us two hours to finally get a total on everything. We had a hundred and twenty pounds of weed, sixty three bricks of cocaine, and seven hundred and forty thousand in cash. I could not believe my eyes. We are set for life, was my thought. All we had to do was get out of town. "We can't stay around here anymore. We gotta leave town."

"Right after we kill Trap!" Benny said. He had to be out of his mind.

"Kill Trap? Is you crazy? They going to kill us if we stay here! It's just you and me Fool!" I wanted him to see that us going against Trap or anybody, would be crazy. We got money and drugs, we set for life, all we had to do is get missing.

"Fuck that, fam! I want blood! They killed my peoples! Our peoples! We gotta hit back!" Benny seethed with rage.

"We just did!" I say as I point to everything around us.

"I want blood!" Benny roared.

"I feel you, but this could lead to our bloodshed! We gotta be smart about this shit! They gon know off top we hit they spot! Nah! We gotta leave!" I say shaking my head thinking about the Mexicans or Chrome and Black, coming looking for us. Hell no, we had to leave town ASAP!

"Mecca! I got to hit Trap. He the reason all this shit went down. He can't live after this." I could see my friend, my brother pleading with me to stay and help him. I was shaking my head, but I knew I would stay and help. "If we do this, we gotta get Trap and then we leave here for good!"

"Bet that up!" Benny exclaimed.

"Call that nigga, set up that meeting you was telling me about." I had this strange feeling running through my body like death was closer than I wanted. Benny was smiling at me looking stupid in the face saying, Niggaz Die Every Day!

* * * * *

"You think them little niggaz is wild like that?" Chrome asked Trap.

"The fool never brought me the truck and he did know where the warehouse was at!" Trap replied.

"I never expected him to bring you the truck, but doubling back to come here and rob the place... that's a surprise. I'm impressed!" Chrome noted.

"I was too, when they hit my spot but now, I'm not. They got to go!" Trap voiced loudly.

"Well, handle your business and Trap, if them little niggaz did have anything to do with this... I'm holding you responsible!" The call ended with Chrome smiling and Trap an unhappy camper.

"Go over to them little niggaz house and rock the damn boat! If they there bring them back to me." The three men Trap spoke to left the room without any questions. After hanging up with Trap, Chrome was still smiling to himself when he dialed Black.

"What's good, cuz?" Black answered.

"Ain't shit, you hear about that warehouse down south?" Chrome asked.

"Yeah, sad story! What you think happened?" Black replied.

"Some young wild ass niggaz made a major move!" Chrome told him.

"Major move?" Black asked, sounding perplexed.

"Well minor in losses but definitely major in principle." Chrome replied.

"So how does the rest of the movie play out?" Black asked, wanting to know more.

"Most likely, the Baldhead one, will save the day." Chrome concluded.

"Oh! I like those kinds of movies! Lots of action, no love stories, or happy endings. Mostly blood, guts, and explosions!" Black sounded like he was looking forward to experiencing how things could unfold.

"Yeah, most heroes are psychos by nature." Chrome noted.

"Let me know when it comes out on DVD! I want to see that one." Black said.

"I heard it went straight to DVD. Available now at all mom and pop stores. Even kids can watch it!" Chrome replied.

"Damn! Imma go get that joint!" Black went on.

"Let me know what you think when you finish!" Chrome told him.

"Truuuuu!" Black was laughing real hard when he ended the call with Chrome. For the first time ever, Chrome wanted the

Baldhead Murderer to do as he pleased. They all knew how the Baldhead got down, so Chrome would tell him to tone it down a little, but not this time. This time, he gave the Baldhead permission to kill at will. This was going to be something to remember, Black thought. He made the call and after replaying the scenario to the Baldhead, Black could hear his smile through the phone. He only had one question... what about Trap?

Chapter Sixteen

* * * * *

We knew Lil G's mom was at work, so we took the cash and the drugs there. We had to bury everything under the dog's house, just so when it was time for us to leave, we could get to it without waking up G's mom. Plus, my main thing was, if Trap or anyone else came looking for us, they would surely think the money was at our houses. As luck would have it, once we came through the door at Benny's house his mother told us some friends came by looking for us. We had no friends alive, so we knew those had to be Trap's people. Right then, I began to get even more nervous than I was before. If they came to Benny's house, I knew they would go to mine. I quickly called my mother and when she answered the phone, I was happy to hear her say that my brother was getting ready for a school dance and no one came by for me. Knowing that my family was safe relaxed me. We needed to get this shit over with quickly before things got out of hand.

"Call Trap!" I told Benny.

"For what?" He asked.

"We need him to stop coming around looking for us!" I demanded.

"I want him to come around while I'm here!" Benny spat back.

"Look OG, Triple OG gangster! Skip all that shit and call this dude. We need to clip his ass and get the fuck from round here!"

I had to watch Benny make the call to Trap. He must've thought this shit was some kind of game. In my mind I'm trying to figure out how we can make this shit all go away. I knew we couldn't just erase everything from our memory, but damn I wanted to get it over with and get far away from Fayetteville as possible.

"You looking for me?" I heard Benny say.

"Ain't nobody running from you. I thought we were going to meet up." Silence for a second.

"That was because I knew you would have come with all your goons ready to kill me, so why would I have showed up." More silence.

"This time, I'm not alone either, so now you can meet me alone. Just you and me, we do the exchange! You bring my money and I'll bring your bullshit greenery." Silence.

"Cool! I'll meet you at the park!"

"Why the hell would you tell him the park?" I asked because I knew the park would be closed for one. So, no one around to stop Trap from killing us and two, it's only one way in and one way out, so we can't run. The park was a dumb idea in my mind.

"Because it's wide open! We can see everyone who comes in. It's one way in--" Benny explained.

"One way out! I know!"

"As soon as it's dark out, we go meet!" Benny said.

"We better get there first. I don't trust that fool!" I was nervous the rest of the day. I had no clue as to what to expect. Anything could happen, anything could go wrong. We had no real plan, and the only thing Benny thought about was killing Trap. Maybe I was just scared or whatever, but I could not see how it was possible that we could just kill Trap and think we were going to get away. It just was not logical.

Around 6:00 pm, we got to the park. It didn't start to get dark until after 6:30 pm. We waited until 7:30 pm, to call Trap and see why he was running so late. Eventually, he came strolling through the lot at 8:00 pm. He was two cars deep! Immediately I told Benny we should leave. I seen movies where the big guys take out the small guys and usually it was because the small guys thought they could outsmart the big guys. Wrong!

"Call him!" Trap told Benny something about he never went anywhere without his protection crew. Fuck That! I snatched the phone from Benny's hand, closed it shut.

"He ain't here to get no weed! They came for us!" I said as I pulled the pistol from my waist.

"We gotta get to him. I'm not leaving here without his head." Benny insisted on going to the grave earlier than I could imagine.

"Ain't no way! It's too many of them!"

"Niggaz Die Every day!" Benny walked away from me. I couldn't believe this shit. I followed him out, towards the parking lot. As soon as we made our presence known, doors from both SUVs opened. Two men from each truck emerged with weapons and I could remember a time when my cousin Perry told me that a scared nigga would shoot you before a real nigga would. Funny as that may be, I knew then how true it was, because I took aim and shot at the first goon I saw. This made all four men duck behind doors as I rained bullet after bullet in their direction. Benny stood beside me shooting as well. We were so far away from them, that our shots could not have been accurate. The only thing that mattered to me was that they were not shooting back at us.

"Let's go!" I shouted to Benny. Somehow, he moved closer to the truck than I had expected him to. The closer he got, the better his shots were. I could see the men who got out the first truck had retreated inside their truck. As for the second, the men were left there as the driver pulled away from Benny. The two guys who were left now out in the open tried to run, but Benny's shots were better and more on target. He was too close to miss. I ran up behind him as the trucks pulled away. I wasted my last few shots, shooting at the trucks that were no longer a problem to us. When the trucks were out of sight, Benny made sure both men were dead. I too pulled the trigger once more, hoping to end the life of those who were already gone. We ran back behind the building where our car sat already started. We left the park not the way it was expected, but through the baseball field, and out through the watermelon patch that grew next to the park. In the morning, some farmer will be upset, but at least we were still alive.

Chapter Seventeen

* * * * *

The Baldhead Murderer was known to take his time killing a man. It was more than a specialty, it was an urge to kill. A desire to see the breath leave the body of his victim. He spent nearly 18 hours working Bug over and over with various tools. The call from Black had interrupted him from using the screwdriver, which was supposed to be inserted into the wounds. Each wound was now packed with dirt, which The Baldhead kept close by so his victims wouldn't bleed out. He had to place the screwdriver down to answer the call, but once he was done, he left the room. There in the basement left alone was Bug, hanging from a pole. The thought of being left there by himself was a relief only because he knew he wouldn't be tortured until The Baldhead returned. Swinging back and forth trying desperately to get loose, Bug thought about his freedom. The thought was shortened, when he heard the door above swing open and then his ears were tickled by the sound of small footsteps coming down the stairs. He was sure The Baldhead was back to finish what he started, but instead... it was a dog. The dog did as it did once before, it came over to him, sniffed once, then sniffed twice, and then walked away to search for some food that was kept in the corner. Bug did not move much, but he made sure to pay attention to the dog's every move.

* * * * *

The drive to Fayetteville took The Baldhead all of five hours. The first thing he did once he got to town was reach out to Trap. His assignment was to make sure that Trap handled his business and, if things weren't done the correct way, he was supposed the get rid of all those in his way. This is what he does. This is what he likes to do. The only thing that could stop The Baldhead from torturing a man, is being able to torture more men. He knew the moment he got to Trap's place that he was going to enjoy his stay in 'The Ville'.

"What are you doing here?" Trap asked The Baldhead as soon as he saw him. It was a known fact, to those who knew, whenever you saw The Baldhead, death was sure to follow, hence the worried look on Trap's face.

"Only here to help!"

"Don't worry bout nothing, we got this all under control." Trap tried to be more confident than he is. Truthfully, The Baldhead's presence concerned him.

"I'm not worried! You should be!" There it was, the message!'

"Nothing to worry about I got this! Right now, my boys bout to go over to the cousins house and find out exactly where they hiding. We gon have them, right here in no time."

"Sounds good but just in case I want to ride along!"

We had to hurry back to Benny's house because we needed to grab everything we were taking with us and bounce. The plan was to leave at midnight, so Benny had to grab some clothes and everything else he wanted to bring along. He also wanted to at least let his mom know he was taking off for a trip across the country. She didn't pay too much attention to the things he did, so she wouldn't notice him gone until that time came when he had been gone too long. I only lived up the street, so I walked home so I could do pretty much the same things. I knew one thing though, we had to be quick and we had to grab the money and drugs from G's house, so I hurried on home. I kissed my mother as passed her in the kitchen. My mouth was dry, so I grabbed me a soda water then went upstairs to shower. I needed to clear my head and then think a bit. Once the shower was done, I laid down across my queen sized bed, closed my eyes, and reflected on tonight's events. The time was 9:15 pm.

Trap made the call to Orlando, to set up a buy. Orlando, being the guy in town who sells the heavy metal, waited patiently for his money to arrive. He knew all about the things his cousin, Benny and Trap had been going through. His motto was, ' I only sell the guns so I'm not responsible for what happens after they were gone.' The only problem with that is, he knew that if Trap thought he was supplying the enemy, Trap would take it personally. This knowledge and the fact that he did not trust anyone, Orlando was strapped. He kept the beretta tucked neatly under his shirt, just in case he needed to protect himself. The head lights from an approaching car told Orlando that his guests had arrived. He let the garage door up and then he waited while three men came his way. He knew two were men he saw around Trap on the regular. The third guy, an unfamiliar face to him. From a distance he could see the shadow of a tall man. He wasn't wide or skinny, but of average build. In the light, Orlando could see the man was bald so he assumed the man was older than the other two, maybe an uncle. The closer they got, Orlando could see the baldness was by choice because the man could not have been older than 33.

"Come on in! How can I help you, my friends?" Orlando greeted them politely. The Baldhead had never been one for too many words. He played the background as Trap's men asked Orlando questions hoping to find out where his cousin could be. As he waited for them to get answers, he took notice to the tools, that were scattered around the garage. In one corner, he saw what looked to be an old air compressor. In another corner, sat a work table. On top of the work table, there were various tools. What took The Baldhead's breath away was the battery-operated handsaw. The circular blade was exposed, as if someone had just changed the blade.

"Look, I called him for you. He's not home. My aunt said so herself, what more can you want from me." Orlando exclaimed to his now unwanted guest.

"What about his friends? Where do they live?" One of Trap's men asked.

"What friends? They all dead! I believe you know that!" he said.

"Not all! Not yet!" The second man sent from Trap said jokingly. He was smiling at Orlando, and his yellow teeth shined brightly, causing Orlando to look away. That was how and when he saw

The Baldhead coming his way. He tried to run but he was stopped by the first goon. The Baldhead reached for Orlando's neck. He grabbed him tightly, squeezing more and more wanting to see his eyes bulge.

"Don't try to speak! It's too late for that!" The Baldhead whispered. He no longer needed to hear anything from Orlando. His death was now the only thing needed. The handsaw, The Baldhead carried in his right hand. He was using his left hand to choke the life out of Orlando. The saw began to roar, and the sound was enough to make Orlando urinate in his pants. The other two men laughed once they saw the piss form around his pants. The smell of piss only made The Baldhead enjoy his kill that much more. He used the saw only to scare Orlando. He had no real intention to use it to cut, but when Orlando reached into his waistline to retrieve a pistol, it caused The Baldhead to react quickly and moved the saw blade across the wrist of Orlando's gun hand. The gun fell to the floor, which made the other two men rush to The Baldhead's aid. He simply motioned for them to back away. Orlando was screaming in pain. This was exactly what The Baldhead wanted. His urges were fed by the screams, by the fear he could see in the eyes of his victims.

"Leave us!" The Baldhead ordered the other two men out.

"Trap told us to stay with you! So do whatever sick shit you bout to do, so we can go grab these niggaz."

The Baldhead was quick for his age. The movement went without notice, by the time the goon realized what had happened, his blood was leaking on to the garage floor. The second goon reacted much quicker, he aimed his weapon at The Baldhead, but he did not pull the trigger.

"What the fuck is you doing?" The second goon asked. At this moment, a scared Orlando was trying his best to crawl away without being seen. The Baldhead gave the man with the gun one long look without words. Then before Orlando crawled completely out of sight, he shot Orlando twice in the back. With the look of cold steel in his eyes, he turned to look at the last goon in the room.

"Where to next?" The next stop was Benny's house. The second goon along with others had been by Benny's house before, but this time, The Baldhead Murderer was with him. They knocked on the door like regular visitors coming to see friends. Only this was no friendly visit. Benny's mother opens the door with a smile, but her smile escaped her as The Baldhead plunged a screwdriver stolen from Orlando's garage into her belly. She tried to scream from the pain but the hand around her mouth muffled her cries. Strongly, The Baldhead pushed and half carried her body to the couch.

Meanwhile, behind him, the second goon closed the front door. They were fast but silent. Each one knowing exactly what to do and who it was they were looking for. Benny sat in his room oblivious to all the things that were going on in his home. He had his music on, happy to be alive, and on his way out of town. The money they kept at G's house, on his mind. He could imagine all the things he would buy. First, he wanted to buy a house, one he and Mecca could live like kings in. Then he wanted to buy himself a nice ride. He liked the Range Rover he saw Chrome driving, so buying one appealed to him. The thought of purchasing a Range Rover from the money he stole from Chrome, was funny to him. He laughed out loud to himself, just as the door to his room opened. The man before him was someone he had never seen before, but the second guy was someone he knew very well.

Chapter Eighteen

* * * * *

Chrome walked through the Harrah's Casino in New Orleans enjoying the excitement that comes along with gambling. A text from one of his girls caught his attention. She told him that she had fifteen hundred for him and this brought a smile to his face. He did not even bother to text her back, he just continued to walk over to the 3-card poker table. He had to put his phone away to play so he pushed it deep into his pocket. He placed the few chips he had left on the table, waiting for the deal to come around his way. So far, the night had been a good night for him. He came to the casino, with three girls and two grand. He now had somewhere around ten grand cash in his pocket and a thousand in chips on the table. He thought about how Trap said, he was being charged twenty grand for the weed that was supposed to be his in the first place. He was laughing at how these young kids could be so daring, even when faced with death. The fact that they tried to get money out of Trap made Chrome wonder if they really had anything to do with the warehouse. It could have been someone else but that could only mean that there was another enemy out there.

The reasonable answer would be that these young niggaz tried they hand by snatching the drugs and money from the warehouse, and then tried to cover things up by asking for money to give back the weed. Maybe, but Chrome had survived thus far by going with his gut and his gut was telling him to end this at all costs. Hence, the real reason he sent The Baldhead Murderer. If anyone could find out the truth, it would be The Baldhead. He had ways of making the toughest men tell him what he wanted to know. What really made The Baldhead efficient was, if he didn't get the information he was looking for, he took much pleasure in killing his prey. This, to Chrome was a gift and a curse, because in some cases, The Baldhead would never ask the much-needed questions. He would rather kill, kill, kill.

Chrome wanted answers which is why he text The Baldhead. When the text came back, TRU INDEED, it was all Chrome needed to see. He knew his childhood friend understood that he wanted answers and The Baldhead would surely have them. The dealer finally dealt him in, he waited until he had all his cards. He took a sneak peek as if someone was behind him looking over his shoulder. He had a three-card flush, all spades, king high. He just looked up at the dealer and smiled slightly. "The King is here!"

* * * * *

Boc...Boc...Boc...Boc! Benny did not waste time on asking why they were there. He decided to let his gun speak for him. In the doorway, The Baldhead fell, and the goon behind him fell as well. Benny grabbed his suitcase and hauled ass out of his room. He had to step over both men but kept on going. He yelled for his mother hoping like hell she was somewhere safe. He made it downstairs where he continued to scream his mother's name. His voice, along with his body, stopped. His heart may have skipped a few beats, looking at his mother's lifeless body spread across the coach. He could see she was gone, her soul somewhere in the next life. Far away from the world she once knew so well.

He allowed his emotions to get the best of him. Even though his mother wasn't the best, she was still his mother, and the thought of losing her to something he done was beginning to eat at him. He ran to her side, rage flowed through him as he caressed his mother's cheek. He started the rise to his feet, his intentions were to run upstairs and put more bullets in those fools heads. He took quick steps towards the stairs, murder on his mind. He was so sure that they were already dead that he wasn't prepared for The Baldhead, who was standing at the top of the stairs. He aimed, but the bullet did not come from his gun, it came from The Baldhead's. The shot was precisely aimed at Benny's thigh. It was not a kill shot, he wanted to cause pain and slow Benny down. Things were moving too fast, and The Baldhead hated to lose control. He took the steps two at a time and shot Benny twice more in the buttocks. Benny's crawl came to an end, as he fell flat on his stomach. He kicked the pistol far away from Benny's reach, and then for no reason other than to cause pain, he shot Benny in the foot.

There was no way Benny could escape his tormentor. H cried silently trying hard to block the pain he felt. He could feel The Baldhead breathing and standing over him. He wanted to look up at him, try to stare his killer in the face when he dies. No such luck was possible. The Baldhead knelt down beside him and casually pulled the trigger again, sending a piece of burning metal through Benny's left shoulder. Then with the strength of three men, he lifts Benny off the floor and then carried him to the car. The keys to the car were with the goon so, knowing that Benny could not escape, he was left in the car.

The Baldhead returned to the house, where he searched the goon's pocket for the keys. He then walked out of the house quietly and nicely closed the door behind himself. Back at Trap's place, he carried Benny to the door and then dropped him to the floor once he was inside. The Baldhead took his time removing the bulletproof vest he wore. Using his fingers to examine the bruises he earned by walking into Benny's room unannounced.

"Where's the others?" Trap asked.

"They did not make it. Do you have somewhere I can talk to him alone?" The Baldhead asked as he played with his new war wounds.

"The basement!" Trap had his men escort The Baldhead along with Benny down to the basement. This basement was a new add on, being that it is not a part of the original house plans. He dug this room for these specific reasons. Those that knew about this room either came to die or they were the ones doing the killing. The Baldhead came down to the basement with his usual bag of tricks. He took the time to remove his special bag from his own car, just so he could get the answers Chrome so desired. The thing with him was he had to make sure that his victims saw the tools as he removed them from the bag. He noticed that Benny was unconscious, so he slapped him hard to wake him up. First item from the bag was a silk scarf, which he made sure that Benny's eyes were open enough to see. He took his time spreading the silk scarf out neatly in front of Benny. The table was nothing more than a fold out card table. One Trap took from the corner and placed in front of Benny to observe. The Baldhead removed all wrinkles from the scarf before he removed the same screwdriver he used on Benny's mom. The screwdriver came from his pocket and the blood could be seen by all those who looked on.

Just to be sure, the Baldhead made it a point to bring the screwdriver within Benny's point of view. He quietly and protectively sat the screwdriver down on top of the silk scarf. The next item he removed from his bag of tricks, was a hammer, one that looked to be brand new, bought just for this occasion. Same routine, the hammer was removed from the bag and then brought in view of Benny's eyes and then placed neatly on the silk scarf. Next, came the butcher's knife. It too, looked to be brand new. It had that Rambo look to it. Benny's eyes closed just a moment, but The Baldhead refused to be denied his moment, so he waited patiently for the eyes to open again. There, in front of him, Benny, saw the butcher's knife, he began to plead for his life.

"Shhh! Don't talk!" The Baldhead warned him. The last item came from The Baldhead's waistline. He then placed the pistol on the scarf, in the same fashion as he did all the other items, Making sure Benny saw each and every one of them. "Where's your friend?" This was the time to talk, but Benny said nothing. The Baldhead kept his eyes on his tools. His fingers slowly gliding over each item as if he was caressing a beautiful woman.

"I want you to understand something about me. I don't care if you answer me at all. Truthfully, I prefer you not to talk! I take a certain pleasure in the kill. It's what calms me! Now I'm going to ask you a few questions, mostly because I have to. If you answer them, I will kill you. If you don't answer them, I will kill you very slowly. Either way, I am going to enjoy taking your life. The air you breathe now is a blessing given to you by your God. The way you stop breathing is on you. Fast or slow!" The Baldhead chose the screwdriver, then gave Benny a view of the blood already there.

"This blood is the blood of the beautiful lady back at your home. I'm sure she was your mother! Soon your blood will be intertwined with hers! Soon the two of you will meet again."

"Fuck you!" Benny screamed.

The Baldhead smiled! "Where's your friend?" Benny said nothing.

"This is where the torture begins!"

Chapter Nineteen

* * * * *

"Benny called while you were sleeping. It sounded like he was crying. Is everything okay?" My mother was at my room door bothering me before I even had the chance wipe the cold out my eyes. How was I supposed to know if everything was alright. Shit, last I checked, everything was better than alright. We have lots of cash and planned to leave town soon. Hell, I'd say everything was just peachy!

"What he say, ma?" I asked.

"I told him I was on the other line with your brother, letting him know to be back here from school on time." She told me.

"What did he want?"

"To see if he could stay out later. I told him no!" She replied.

"Not him! I'm talking about Benny, ma!"

"How am I supposed to know? I told him to call back!" I left my mother at my room door and hurried to the house phone. I wanted to know what Benny had wanted and if so, why was he crying. When I received no answer, I began to worry. "What's going on?" She demanded to know.

"Nothing, ma!" Neither of us had our cellphones, but we purchased cheap phones earlier before we tried Trap at the park, but I did not know the cell number. I tried the caller ID but, whatever phone Benny used had a blocked number. Since we only live down the street from each other, I got dressed and walked down to his house. I was happy to see his car was in the driveway so I knew then he had to be sleep. I knocked twice on the door, but received no answer. I tried knocking again, this time a lot harder and louder than before. Still, no one came to the door. Being that I could see through the window, I took a peek, and I could clearly see Benny's mother on the couch.

She was sleeping, so that fact alone when I knocked again, I knocked a lot softer than the last time. Since no one came to the door, I assumed everyone had to be sleep. I did what we did most of the times went snuck out the house, I went to his window, which was around the back. I threw a few rocks at the window hoping to wake him up, but nothing. I continued to reach Benny by throwing rocks until I grew bored and gave up. I then jumped the fence, heading over to Lil G's yard. I had skip over two sets of fences but then I was in G's backyard. I was telling myself he wouldn't do it, but I wanted to make sure Benny didn't take the money and drugs and bounce without me. That would be foul! I located the shovel exactly where we left it. That within itself should have told me my homeboy was still on the up and up, but I continued to check anyway. It did not take long for me to start seeing the plastic of the hidden treasures below. I knew Benny had not been there, so I replaced the dirt, covering the hole back up. I fed the dog before I left and then jumped my way back to

Benny's yard. Coming over the last fence, I saw a car leaving from Benny's driveway.

That's this nigga right there... I said to myself. I watched the car back out and leave. I came through the fence just before the car hit the corner leaving the block. I checked the door once more, knocking and no one came, so I left. I was coming through the door and my mother told me Benny called again. Now, I'm more worried than I was before but what was even more crazy was the fact that she said some friends of mine just came by. The fact that she told me that she explained to them that I just walked down to Benny's house would explain the car I saw leaving his driveway. Trap's people! I knew eventually they would come looking for us, since we did shoot up their cars and pretty much stole the weed. *Serves them right,* I thought. I was now convinced Benny was somewhere hiding out trying to reach me so we could leave. They keep coming to our houses, so we had to leave town quickly.

"Did Benny say anything this time?" I asked.

"No! I told you, he sounds like he's crying. What's going on?" Again, she wanted to know.

"Nothing, ma!" I started to walk back out the door, but she stopped me.

"Where you going? I need you to go get your brother from the school." She ordered me.

"Ma, why you can't go get him?"

"Boy!" She snapped.

"Alright, ma I'll go get him. Where's the keys?" She told me where the keys were, I grabbed them then told her, "If Benny calls back, tell him I went to the school so to meet me here, at the house."

"You gon stand here and act like nothing's wrong when you know good and well I raised your poe butt! I know when you lying and when you telling the truth." She retorted.

"What?" I shrugged my shoulder as if to fake like nothing extra was going on, but inside I was shaking badly. My nerves were bad, but I wouldn't let my mom catch wind of it.

Life is too short... She went on and on about this and that. Seriously, I blocked her out from the first word. My mind was on finding Benny and getting the hell away from Fayetteville. I sat there listening to her tell me off. There wasn't much I could say back to her, I knew she was right. I had recently lost two friends due to violence, and third friend that no one even knew about. Bug had gone missing, and we never explained anything to anyone about his whereabouts. His family never asked and we never went over there to explain. My mother knew all things about us and was now just blabbing on and on about us not living right. I just wanted her to shut up so I could go get my brat of a brother and get gone from this place.

"Ma, ain't nothing going on! We good!" I had to pretty much interrupt her speech.

"Whatever, boy! Go get your brother and don't be speeding in my car." She said.

"I won't!" I hurried on out the door to the car. As soon as I was away from my mom's disapproving eyes, I did exactly what she told me not to. I started speeding!

* * * * *

I came through the school's parking lot on what felt like two wheels. Looking around made me remember all those days me and my crew would skip school to be with girls and or sell drugs. Those days we had fun. Damn, I miss my crew! I really needed to find Khafil and get back home.

"Hey! You know Khafil?" I asked some random teenager.

"Yeah, he left already!"

Damn! I came out here for nothing. I took one last look around the parking lot, hoping to see Khafil with some chicks or with some friends. I did not see him, so I assumed he did in fact leave. I came down my block in a hurry. Stopping at Benny's house once again hoping he was home. Sure enough, he was not, so I slowly drove home. I didn't want my mother to think I was speeding.

"Where's your brother?" My mother asked me as soon as I came through the door alone.

"They told me he had left already! Calm down, ma! What could Mr. Innocent, get into. Call his cell phone, see where he at."

"I did, already! He never picked up!" She yelled.

"Trust me, ma! He's fine! Did Benny call back?"

"No!" I left my mother in the living room waiting for my little brother to show up. I had much more important things on my mind. I needed to find Benny before shit hit the fan and we both be staring down the barrel of Trap's gun.

Chapter Twenty

* * * * *

I was still trying to figure out a way to find Benny, when my mother's scream caught my attention. The first thing I thought about was the bullshit I've done. I quickly reached for the pistol I kept hidden in my suitcase, that I planned to leave with. I was walking fast like, more like a skip run. The whole time I'm wondering what else could go wrong. The tears crept down her face, so I knew whatever it was, it had to be serious. I hated to see my mother cry. I hated it so much I began to shed tears.

"What's wrong, ma?" Was a question I would never forget. The answer even more so, but the pain I saw in her eyes had nothing on the pain I felt when she slapped me. "What I do?"

"Your brother is dead!" She screamed.

"Dead?" I was confused, hurting and most of all I was in denial. I did not want to believe what I was thinking. Not my brother! There had to be some kind of mistake. Khafil had to be somewhere with his friends and someone who looks like my kid brother must be dead.

"I just spoke with the police. They found his body with his school ID in his wallet. They told me there was message written in blood, across his shirt!"

"A message?"

"I want my money!" She cried. She slapped me again and I fell backwards onto her bed completely stunned by the news, not the assault.

"I know you had something to do with this happening. Benny calling here crying and shit!" She was yelling at me. Her nose runny, and the tears were causing her voice to break.

"You gon tell the police everything you know when they get here. Damn it! And when you done, you get your no-good ass out my house! You hear me!" She was talking to me like I was some stranger on the street. Like I wasn't the same kid who was delivered through her pussy. As if I wasn't the same boy who she breastfed. My own mother looked at me like I was the worst piece of shit on the planet. To say I was hurt would be putting it plain. My emotions were everywhere, and I wanted nothing more than to run to my room and cry. It was like the weight of the world was on my shoulders. All I could do was try to mourn my brother and figure out what my next move would be. Death was here again staring at me, but telling me not you, just those around you. Nothing I did seemed to directly affect me. It was as if death was afraid of me. I caused my brother's death and now my mother wants nothing to do with me. Damn! I cried and I cried. I actually cried until I couldn't cry no more. I spent so much time crying, that I almost missed the police car pull into my driveway.

From my room window, I could see that it was the boy Cedric and another cop. Most likely someone else who was a part of Trap's team. I was not going to lead to my doom, so I crept out my bedroom before they reached the door. I then snuck out the back door and from my backyard I escaped over the fence. There is a path that leads to my old school, next to my house, so I hid there. I knew my mother had to identify the body and most likely that would be why they were there but seeing Cedric made me cautious. It took them twenty minutes to exit my home, no doubt probably looking for me. Even though I watched them all leave in the same car, I waited twenty more minutes before I went back to my house. I never knew when my mom came back home that night. I was just in my room not wanting to leave my bed. In the morning when I woke up, I knew Benny was dead too. It was only a matter of time before I was dead as well.

I had to get away quick, so I did what I thought was best. I looked over at the clock, it was 6:14 am. I knew my mother was fast asleep. I crept out of my bed and hurried out the front door. Outside, I looked in every direction hoping not to see anyone that I consider to be a threat. After no threats were confirmed, I ran all the way to Lil G's house. I tiptoed through his back yard. I found the shovel exactly where I left it the night before. I dug up everything, the money and the drugs. I had to stuff everything inside my suitcase, tossing clothes so the illegals could fit. When I was done, I refilled the hole and then fed the dog. I took extra precaution walking back passed my house to reach the path.

Once I was in the woods, I speed walked to the gas station and had the lady behind the counter call me a cab. The long wait for the cab was very excruciating. Every car that drove by I tried to hide my face from. Every loud noise, I ducked thinking a bullet was heading in my direction. Paranoia would best describe my recent behavior. It was one thing to be worried about Trap, him I'm sure I could have come up with a plan to get away from. Now, I'm sure my problems have gotten way worse, because I'm sure Chrome and Black was now certain I robbed the warehouse. *I want my money!* That had to be them. Killing my brother was a big mistake, one I'm going to make them pay dearly for. It was very early in the morning, so most people were sleeping. I knew people like Trap were in bed tucked away, therefore I had the cab driver take me right to Trap's house. On my mind was murder and mayhem. I paid the cabbie for his assistance and then I watched him pull off. I had to carry my suitcase over to the front door and left it next to the steps. I then did what most uninvited guest would do. I tried the knob, hoping it would open. Just like in the movies, the door opened without any interruptions. I took one last look at my suitcase, not wanting to leave it all alone.

Ready to get to the action, I removed the loaded pistol from my waist. Inside the house was quiet as hell, slightly dark but my eyes were seeing everything. I crept slowly through the house, neither closing the front door, or even caring about who saw me come inside. The first room was the living room in which I saw two dudes deep into their sleep. I passed them by because I wanted to reach the kitchen first. In my mind, I saw myself cutting throats, and living bodies for the cops to sort out. This, of course, was how I was seeing things at the time, not knowing how far gone I truly was. In the kitchen, I found exactly what I was looking for. I removed the big ass steak knife from the sink. They ate good that night before so I knew their stomach matter would have lots to spill. I then crept back into the living room slowly and quietly, I took the first man by the mouth and stabbed the knife deep into his throat. I had to really hold his mouth tight because he was squirming too much, and I was afraid he would wake the goon next to him up. Seeing the life leave his body, made me more than happy, I was lost within myself. I snapped.

Again, I repeated the same technique with the next goon, but my hold on his mouth wasn't as tight as the last guy. He bit my hand, causing me to wince. I swung the knife wildly in his direction, catching him in the chest. He screamed from the pain and reached for the blade, trying painfully to take the knife from me. I pulled the blade out slicing his hand in the process and rammed it back into him again. More screams. They were even louder than the first. Anyone who was asleep now had to be awake. I pulled the knife out again and I wasn't sure of what to do with the blade, so I stuck him again and then again, making sure he was dead. I searched through the first guy's pockets, then through the second guy's pants pockets, until I realized the keys were on the table. I was trying like hell to hurry up because I did not know who else was in the house.

Even though I was committing these murderous acts, I was still nervous. It was like hearing my mother cry and knowing my brother died because of me was too much. I needed to find Trap and make him pay for all that has been done. I knew most of this was my fault, I, along with my crew started this mess, but the line had been crossed and there is no turning back. I had the knife in my right hand, the gun in my left, and the keys, I hoped belonged to one of the cars outside, in my pocket. I hurried up the stairs to the first room I came to. There was no one. The second room, there was one male on the bed. I hopped on the bed straddled the guy so he couldn't move, and to my surprise, it wasn't Trap. It was the loudmouth faggot that had something to say the day we left for VA. The day things all changed for us. His loudmouth then, was saved by Chrome, but there was no one to save his ass now.

"Where's Trap?" I asked him but the fool tried to maneuver me off him, so I went all Michael Myers on his ass. I stabbed that fool at least ten times. Blood covered me like I was playing with red body paint. The shit was so sticky, but I didn't care and continued searching all the other rooms. Eventually, I realized Trap was not there. I was disappointed to say the least, but I had no time to debate the facts. I had to go! There was so much blood all over me, that I had to change my clothes which I took from my suitcase. Leaving the bloody clothes inside with the rest of the crime scene made sense to me. Happy that I made no noise that would alarm any nosy neighbors, I walked outside to kindly find out which car the keys I stole, belonged to.

Once I found my ride, I went back inside, snatched up my suitcase, placed it in the trunk and then went back inside the house. I found any and everything I could, that would help me burn the place down. My objective was to burn all evidence of me ever being there and to send Trap a big 'Fuck You' message. I hoped like hell the whole place burned to the ground, but again I had no time to waste. I lit fires in different places inside the house. Making sure they began to grow and would continue to grow, then I walked outside, entered the car and drove away slowly. I know I didn't find the man I was looking for, but for now I had to go. Trap could not have known how killing my brother would make me a silent beast. They have created the exact enemy they should have hoped to kill, but I'm alive and revenge is so sweet. It's like some good wet pussy and I love some pussy. I remember when I told The Crew, Niggaz Die Every Day, not me! Not today! I somehow have survived time and time again, not only for revenge but LIVE TO DIE ANOTHER DAY!

Chapter Twenty-One

* * * * *

The return home was bittersweet for The Baldhead. His house was nice and quiet, the one thing he loved most. His dogs were on guard as they should be and upon his arrival, they came to him following him inside the home. First thing through the door was the third dog. The Baldhead left him in the house to guard a dead man, who wasn't exactly dead but most definitely on the verge of dying. Walking past the closed basement door, The Baldhead felt the need to open the door, the smell of death usually lingers. He did as he always did, he entered the kitchen to feed his dogs. Then after that he made his way to the bedroom, where he disrobed. He was in a desperate need of a shower. He longed to feel the cold water touch his body, cleansing him from the evils that were his past. In Fayetteville, he spent most of his time hunting and killing, so he had no time for showers. What he did have time for, was effective enough to get the answers Chrome requested but not so effective enough to capture all those held responsible. He shook his head because he knew it should have been done right the first time.

They had Mecca and his friend in VA. He told Black that they should kill both men. Leave no witnesses was his everyday motto, but for some odd reason Black chose to play the game wrongly and now this Mecca character has come back to haunt them. Even still, every man has a weakness and soon The Baldhead would find out if the mother was that weakness. Taking the life of one's brother could cause such a man to break.

No one would give up Mecca's whereabouts. The young brother took death in stride only closing his eyes and crying loudly but he never spoke a word against his brother. The friend Benny, helped out in ways, but held strong in others. For one, he came out with all the information involving the warehouse heist. The Baldhead gave that info to Chrome. Benny tried hard to protect his friend by not telling where he could be found but The Baldhead, by way of phone calls answered by Mecca's mom, knew that Mecca would pick up his little brother at the school. With this information, and Benny begging and pleading him not to, The Baldhead went to the school to intercept Mecca but instead, he took Khafil and left his body in the streets with a message. The message in blood, *I want my money!* Benny wouldn't say where the money and drugs could be found, and nothing was where Trap sent his people to check. All in all, Benny tried to help himself by talking, but he died exactly how Chrome predicted. His throat was slit from ear to ear. Entering the shower, with the water nice and cold, The Baldhead relaxed and felt happy to be home. Too much time on the streets could cause any man to become stressed. He took his time allowing the water to fall down his body and relax his muscles. He spent thirty minutes scrubbing his body hard. There was no blood to be seen or unseen on him. He was just one of those particular people in some ways. He scrubbed and scrubbed, leaving his body red and sore by the time he was done. After the shower, he decided to make himself something to eat. Thinking about those he killed always had a way of making him hungry.

Each recent kill, still fresh on his mind, successfully fulfilling the urges he felt. It took him a little over an hour to finishing cooking himself some fried chicken with mac and cheese. His dogs were trained to his liking so as he sat down to eat, they left the kitchen and escaped to the basement. Over the course of his meal, he reminisced over the way the eyes lost all their luster when the soul left the human body. Most people closed the dead eyes, but The Baldhead left them open. He thought that he could see the afterlife through the eyes of the dead. Those same eyes thought to be the windows of one's soul, to him, were a secret passageway only he knew exist. He would spend hours looking through the eyes of his victims, looking for answers from afar.

In his basement, he was free to do as he pleased to those he chose to be his victims. He entertained the thought that he was God and he believed that he controlled all that crossed his threshold. Reviling in the moment, brought a sense of pride in him. That same sense of pride quickly floating out into the empty space called air, as he remembered his dog being inside the house when he came home. He could remember exactly how he left the dog in the basement and closed the door behind him as he left. He pushed himself away from the kitchen table. Immediately he used his keypad to close and lock all windows and doors. The sound of the window shutters closing over each window could be heard loudly crashing down. He took cautious steps towards the kitchen closet where he kept a shotgun. Removing the shotgun, he then walked to the basement door and slowly took his decent. Before reaching the bottom step, he yelled out the command that would cause his dogs to attack all strangers. The growls of vicious animals could be heard. To his left, he could see broken glass on the floor. To his right he saw that the so-called dead man wasn't dead at all. In fact, he was pretty much alive! So alive, that he was gone! The glass came from a window so small, he knew that no man could squeeze out. This only meant his victim walked out the front door. This piece of information disturbed him so, that he took aim and shot all three of his dogs. The buck shot shells spread, thus catching two of the dogs squarely. The second shot caught all three. The third shot ensured that they all were dead. He would have to get more later, and train them a lot better than these. Breathlessly, he had to carry them one by one to the furnace. One at a time, he watched them burn. The smell of death mixed with the burning flesh and hairs of a dog consumed him. One by one, he watched them burn. One by one, he fueled his urge!

Epilogue

* * * * *

T alk about nerve-racking, the actual wait for the bus to leave, was worse than taking a man's life. I was half expecting the police, half expecting Trap or anyone of his peoples to climb aboard and force me off. No one came, and I couldn't have been any happier once the wheels of the bus went round and round. From the Greyhound bus window, I watched the city I grew up in go pass me. The many things I've done in the city all were now behind me. Travelling on 95N gave me the opportunity to grieve those who were dead and gone. Throughout my short time of living, I have lost so many friends and family, people who I would have gave my own life to save. People I would have gladly switched places with.

Thinking this over made the tears turn into rage and that rage is what gave me the strength I needed to take life so easily. What was it about me that kept me alive? A question I could not answer, but one that circled my thoughts time and time again. Why my brother? So young was he and to think it was all my fault. Foolish! But never again! This time when I strike I was going to be in the shadows. I was not going to let them see me coming. I was going to take my revenge! Systematically crushing everything that they built, leaving them to wonder if it's me or someone else. Richmond, VA was a hold over stop for me. I took the two-hour layover to do some shopping. I bought myself a little carry-on suitcase, one I could store my cash a lot better. I kept the drugs inside the bigger suitcase, just in case! I also bought myself some new clothes. Back at the Greyhound station, I arrived on time to hear my bus being reloaded. Glad to be on my way, I hurried to the gate to load with the others. This trip was short, Washington, DC wasn't far at all. The plan was to get to DC, then buy another ticket to somewhere west. I dragged my luggage over to the line, which was a lot longer than I expected. On the way to this line, I was approached twice by homeless men who wanted to help me with my bags. Too much to lose, so I declined any assistance.

After retrieving my ticket, I found the gate I was supposed to wait at. Not even five minutes after I was seated, did another homeless man walk up to me. I was already on my feet, hands quickly grabbing my suitcase in case this one tried to snatch and run. The closer he got, the more his face became familiar to me. I had gotten rid of the knife, threw the gun down the sewage drain and here it was I was unarmed and afraid.

"I thought you were dead!" he said.

"Me? I thought you were dead!" I replied.

"I should be!"

"What the fuck? How?" I asked.

"I escaped!" I pulled the homeless man, who wasn't at all homeless, in for a brotherly hug. I was elated to see his face again.

I was no longer alone. Together we would be a problem! Together, we would avenge our crew!

"So, what you saying? This little nigga just gets a pass?" Trap had asked Chrome this for the third time. He found out shortly after Mecca arrived at Richmond, that his men were killed in an attempted fire. The house never caught fire like Mecca thought. The bodies within the house were discovered, and homicide detectives had determined the scene to be staged. These lead detectives had to call in a forensic team and none of this made Trap happy. Even Cedric was unable to help. The whole scene has placed Trap on Fayetteville's finest, watch list. He was furious about it all.

"I'm not saying that anyone gets a pass. I'm just saying, Niggaz Die Every Day, the police know that, you know that. In due time, we will find this fool! Until then, you need to take a fucking vacation!" Chrome said.

"A vacation? Where the fuck would I go?" Trap asked.

"I don't care where you go or where you don't go!" Chrome barked.

"So, what you saying?" Trap pressed on.

"I believe I said it loud and clear!" Chrome barked again.

"How bout you say it even clearer for me! You know us southerners a little slower than you New Yorkers!" Trap jabbed.

"Be careful!" Chrome warned.

"Be careful?" Trap asked.

"Yeah! Be careful!" Chrome went on. "Because we wouldn't want you to say something you would regret later. Cause we both know Niggaz Die Every Day!"

Live by It, Die By It (By: Ice Money)

Live By It, Die By It 2 (By: Ice Money)

Mercenary (By: Ice Money)

The Ruler of the Red Ruler (By: Kutta)

The Trenches: Murder, Money, Betrayal (By: Kutta)

Block Boyz (By: Juvi)

Da $treets Raised Me & Da Guns Paid Me (By Juvi & Splash Queen)

Team Savage (By: Ace Boogie)

Team Savage 2 (By: Ace Boogie)

Team Savage III (By: Ace Boogie)

Love Have Mercy (By: Kordarow Moore)

Rich Pride (By M.L. Moore)

Available at Bagzofmoneycontent.com and most major bookstores.

Made in United States
Orlando, FL
20 March 2023

31234891R00070